United Way
of Portage County

www.uwportage.org

WAITING FOR EUGENE

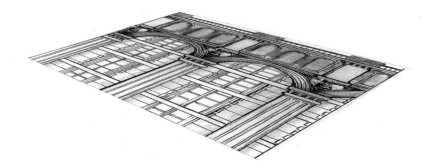

Fic
Lowenstein

Published by
Lion Stone Books
4921 Aurora Drive
Kensington, MD 20895
U.S.A.

First Edition
10 9 8 7 6 5 4 3 2 1

Cataloging-in-Publication Data
Lowenstein, Sallie
Waiting For Eugene/Sallie Lowenstein
p. cm.

Summary: Twelve year old Sara Goldman wins the chance to study
art for a summer in New York City, but she must first sort through her
father's war-torn childhood stories to help him find his way out of the past.

ISBN: 0-9658486-55
[1. Art–Fiction 2. War/Holocaust–Fiction
3. Mental Illness–Fiction   4. Father/Daughter–fiction]

Library of Congress Control Number: 2004096654

Printed in China

WAITING FOR EUGENE

Sallie Lowenstein

Lion Stone Books

"Grant us peace, your most precious gift..."
The New Union Prayerbook

"Our lives and architecture fuse as a continual metamorphosis of
being and becoming... a joyful dance between
polarities and paradoxes..."
Gregory Burgess

This book is for those of us who must create, and is especially dedicated to
my daughter, Rachel Kenney.

AT SUMMER'S FALL

Artichokes and Green Okra

The door was open just enough for me to see that Papa had pulled the heavy curtains across the windows of his study again, blocking all but a few lonely threads of sunlight that managed to creep in at the edges. His voice was barely audible from inside the darkened room, yet I could hear it trembling.

"*Thrump, thrump. Thrump, thrump.* Their boots pound on our staircase."

I pushed the door open a little more and watched as he walked the edge of the room.

"Papa?" I asked uneasily.

He stopped and turned his ear towards where I stood so that the dim light caught his profile in silhouette. "Closer, closer! *Thrump. Thrump.* They're coming! Quick, under the bed, *Sara.* Hide!" he cried out. "No, wait! Monsters lurk there—in the dust, waiting to eat us." He pulled at his hair as he looked frantically around the room. "But, there is nowhere else to hide! Nowhere but under the bed."

Backing up, he pressed himself into a corner and squatted, as if to make himself as small as possible.

"Papa! Please, Papa, it's okay!" I whispered and stepped into the shadowy light.

"No! Do not speak! Shssh! Do not breathe. Maybe the soldiers won't find us here in the dust with the monsters. Ssshh. Not a sound! Not a breath!"

I gingerly reached out and took his hand. Up close I could see wrinkles and creases in his shirt and pants.

"Papa, It's me, Sara! Don't you know me?"

"*Thrump, thrump,*" he whispered.

"Now Michel, don't you scare your daughter!" Mama called out sharply as she passed by his study.

He blinked at the sound of her voice and looked up at me with the wide eyes of a startled deer, then in a single motion, rose and sat in his desk chair.

"Sara, my daughter?"

"Yes, Papa, your daughter. Who else would I be?"

"My little Sara," he said with a sigh, and absently plucked me into his lap as if I were still small. It was good he knew who I was, but chills still crawled down my spine as he held me.

"My *grand-maman* was the first they took, Sara."

"Who took her, Papa?"

"They came. Turned out the lights. Skewered *tous les enfants et tous les grands-parents.*"

He stroked my head as in my mind I nervously went over the foreign words to be sure of what he had said.

His voice hushed when he spoke again. "Sometimes I try to remember what the *grand-maman* looked like. Was her hair white? Was she the one with paper-thin, blue skin? I cannot remember anymore."

"Don't you have a picture of her?"

He rubbed his eyes and winced. "They burned all our pictures. I have left only what I carry in my head."

"Maybe your sisters have pictures, Papa."

He stood, setting me on my feet as he stalked off silently.

Mama was standing by the doorway and beckoned me to her. She put her arm around my shoulders and, as if speaking to herself, said, "None left."

Before I could ask her what she meant, she patted the small of my back and sent me off in the direction of the back door. "Go on and play, Sara."

As I stepped through the door, I thought I heard a voice say, *Go have fun, while you can.*

Willie was already hanging out the window of his tree house by the time I got outside.

"Wanna come up?" he asked.

"What about your gang? Aren't they coming today?"

"No, they all gotta go to church."

That was good. I didn't much like the boys who usually held reign over Willie's tree house, and I wasn't in the mood to deal with them. I climbed the ladder, listening to my shoes clunk on the rungs until I reached the platform.

"How's your dad today?" he asked me. "Any better?"

I shrugged. So far, today was a bad day for Papa. Today he was reliving his stories. Mama and my Nana said Papa was suffering from delusions. They claimed his memories were all tangled up, all mixed up with make-believe.

"So, did he tell you any more of his tales?"

"Why do you wanna know, Willie?" I asked. "Is that why you invited me up here, so I could tell you more stories?"

"Of course not, but they are kinda interesting."

"Well, I don't have any new ones. Papa's just sad today."

I closed my eyes to keep back the tears. It seemed to me Papa had been sick forever this time. It was getting harder and harder to remember what he was like when he was well. A piece of a picture here, a piece there. A flash of a smile. A butterfly perched on his big hand. His fingers wrapped gently around mine.

"Hey, don't cry," Willie said. "I'm sorry."

"Yeah, yeah." I wiped at my eyes and sniffled. I didn't want to talk about Papa, so before Willie could ask me what was wrong, I asked him quickly, "Who do you think you're gonna get for seventh grade English?"

"With my luck I'll get old Mr. Yankers. My sister says he's *awful*," Willie said, pulling the last word out as he shivered all over at the thought.

It made me laugh to watch him. Willie was chubby, and when he shivered he reminded me of a wiggly bowl of Jell-O, which made me remember a story. Before I could stop myself, I said, "Hey, Willie, did I ever tell you Papa's story about Buffy the cat?"

"Nope."

"Well, I'll tell you just this one story."

Willie waited attentively, his eyes glued to me. There was nothing for it now, but to start.

"When Papa first came to this country, the lady he lived with had a cat named Buffy who was scared of just about anything that moved. Strange people, a mouse, a cockroach, all sent Buffy into hiding.

"Buffy weighed nearly thirty pounds and ate everything, absolutely everything! When Papa left part of a peanut butter sandwich on a plate, Buffy gulped it down. When someone left artichoke heart salad out—swallow, snap, just like that." I snapped my fingers.

"My cat wouldn't touch that stuff!" Willie exclaimed.

"Wouldn't catch me eating artichoke hearts, either," I said, "but Buffy chomped down everything, even avocado and okra!"

"Nah, not okra! No cat would eat okra!" Willie protested.

I ignored his comment. "One day Papa saw Buffy eyeing a green Jell-O mold sitting out on a platter. Buffy jumped up on the counter, put his nose near the Jell-O and sniffed. The mold wiggled a tiny bit and Buffy's whiskers twitched. He tested the Jell-O with a paw and of course the Jell-O shook all over. The split second it did, Buffy panicked. He jumped back, raked the jiggling Jell-O with his claws, and brushed over a stack of dishes with his tail. Crash! His fur stood straight up like in a cartoon, and he dashed under the couch as fast as he could. Papa didn't glimpse one whisker of Buffy for three whole days!"

"You mean that cat didn't eat anything for three days?" Willie asked skeptically.

"Not that Papa saw. When Buffy came out, he still ate peanut butter cookies and chocolate cake, just like before, except..."

I paused for emphasis, waiting for Willie to take the bait, just as Papa had waited when he told me the story.

"Except what?" Willie asked.

"Except, Buffy never ate anything green again—not olives, or avocado, or asparagus, or lettuce, or..."

"Aw, you're joshing me!" Willie interrupted.

"Am not!" I said straight-faced.

Willie shook his head hard. "Anyways, I didn't wanna hear a story about a mangy old, fat cat. I wanted one of the ones your father tells when he's really crazy."

I stood up and clunked my head on the ceiling. "My Papa's not crazy at all! You take that back!"

"Okay, okay, I'm sorry. Maybe he isn't crazy, but you gotta admit, some of his stories are!" Willie said.

"Well, that doesn't make him crazy! I'm going home!" I climbed down the ladder as fast as I could and ran back into my own yard.

I dropped down into the grass, balled up my fists and rubbed at my eyes. My Papa told wonderful stories. The problem was, he mainly told them to me when he was sick. I felt a tear roll down my cheek. When Papa was well, he didn't tell many stories. When he was well, he was very proper; very tidy; and dressed so neatly; and stood so straight. Mama said he was an Architect of Stature when he was well. I wiped at the tear angrily. I hated it when he was sick, but it didn't keep me from loving his stories, except for the scary ones. I wished he didn't tell me the ones when it was dark and he was hungry and no one came to feed him, or even bring him water. When those unbidden tales rose out of him, fear seemed to seep out of every one of his pores like sweat, but I sat through them, trying not to let his terror leach into me, because mixed into them were the other stories, the wondrous ones that Willie wanted to hear.

I got up from the ground, brushed off my shorts and walked inside. Mama was in the kitchen stirring chocolate chips into cookie dough.

"I don't wanna play outside anymore, Mama."

"No? Well, do you want to help me make cookies? I'm ready to drop them onto the trays."

"Sure! Can I lick?"

I began to push the dough off the spoon into bumpy lumps studded with chips. Mama took the tray when I was done and slid it into the oven.

"How old was Papa when the war came?" I asked her.

"Nine or ten."

"How old was his sister?"

"Which one? The baby was eleven months or so, and his other sister, she was maybe eight."

"Why don't we go visit them sometime, Mama?"

Mama's eyes caught mine in an amazed stare. "Sara, they're all dead."

I dropped the spoon filled with cookie dough on the floor.

"But Papa never talks like they're dead!" Goose bumps were racing up and down my arms and legs.

Mama bent down to wipe up the mess and handed me the spoon. "Sara, I thought you knew." She straightened up and pushed my hair out of my face. "You're twelve, surely you knew!"

"No, I didn't!"

"But Sara, wouldn't we visit them if they were alive?"

"I just thought Europe was too far away for visits, that's all! I didn't know!"

"I'm so sorry, Sara, but they died long ago in the war."

Skewered by the soldiers, was what sped through my mind, but what I said was, "You mean they were killed?"

She reached out, took me into her arms and rocked me.

"They can't be dead, Mama. They can't be!"

"The only one who survived was your father."

How could they be gone? Papa's little sisters? His mother? His father? They couldn't all have died in the war! Hadn't he told me stories about them when it was over; when they were together again; when he didn't have to hide anymore? Hadn't he?

Suddenly I didn't want Mama to hold me. I wished I didn't know! I wished she hadn't told me! I tried to push away from her embrace, but she held me tight. I tried to hit her, but she just hugged me harder.

"Sara, listen to me. All that time when your father was hidden under the barn floor, it made him sick."

"Then why'd you marry him?" I screamed and broke free.

She grabbed me again and held me as I sobbed. Her voice was soft and sad when she spoke. "It was an awful time. The war took so many people. Families were decimated. Some people had nothing left. I was sixteen when I saw your father for the first time at my school. He was so skinny and pale that I thought he was ugly. A skeleton cloaked in skin. But your papa, he had a light in his eyes that caught my attention, as if he knew something no one else did."

I knew that look. He had it when he told me the stories.

"He was funny and he told me about lovely places he had seen and exotic people he had known, and he never mentioned any of the horror. I thought he was wonderful, so full of all things wonderful." A deep sigh escaped her.

"He is!" I said.

She released me and asked, "Yes? I'm glad."

But the look in her eyes said something else. The look in her eyes was like an apology.

I ran out of the room, up the stairs, and threw myself onto my bed, sobbing and pummeling my mattress, but it didn't make me feel any better, and when I looked up Papa was standing in the hall watching me.

"What's the matter, Sara?" he asked.

I rolled over and rubbed my nose on my sleeve. "Who did you play with while you were hiding?"

"Oh," he said, almost buoyantly, "so many playmates! One of my favorites was a little black-haired fellow who couldn't have been four feet tall, but claimed he was fifteen years. He was the best *constructeur de maisons* I ever met. He could dig in the dirt, just ordinary dirt, and build the most dazzling castles!"

"Even in the little bit of light that filtered into the hole through the barn floor?" I asked him.

"Yes, even then!"

"How many of you hid under the barn?"

He thought a minute, moving his fingers up and down as if counting. "Well, some came and some went and then others came, but maybe twenty-five or thirty of us altogether."

I slapped at a late-summer mosquito before I asked, "Why was the digger hiding?"

"He never told me."

"Why were you down there, Papa?"

He continued the story as if I hadn't asked the question. The only change was he began to pace as he spoke. "*Le Constructeur* had long, finely pointed nails, painted thickly with blue enamel to make them tough so he could dig better."

Papa walked right up to my bedroom wall and pivoted to pace in the other direction.

"Once he built a whole castle! It had turrets and serpentine walls, and with the tips of his nails he etched little faces in the windows." He turned and paced the other way again. "He said the prince in the high tower was me! He kept on digging and digging, until he had made such a huge castle there was hardly any room left for us to move about in. It was amazing, all the twists and turns, the steps and the staircases, the towers and the rooms he made."

"What happened to it?"

He stopped and stood still. "Oh, someone new came, and we had to demolish it so there was room for another person."

"Dinner," Mama called from downstairs.

"Come now, Sara," Papa said.

As we walked down the steps, he suddenly squared his shoulders, and straightened his shirt, and raised his head. The Architect of Stature walked ahead of me and took his place at the table.

"Now then," he said, "what are the plans for tomorrow?"

Dust Balls and Shopping Trips

In the morning, Papa shaved and combed his hair. He put on a stiff shirt and a dark blue tie and went down to his study. He stood perfectly still in the center of the room for a while before he slowly, slowly, pulled the curtains away from the window panes and let in the summer sun. He ran his hands over his hair and let his fingers linger at his cheeks, then he opened his file drawers and pulled out a project to work on.

"Close the door, Sara," he said without looking up. "I've work to do."

"Let's go shopping," Mama called from the kitchen. "It's a beautiful day. We can walk, and if you bring your suit, on the way back we can go swimming."

"Mama, could we go to the park instead? I'll bring my sketchbook and my pencils."

She nodded and I raced up the stairs to my room. I was about to leave when I remembered that one of my good pencils had rolled under the bed. It was way at the back. I lay on my belly and squirmed under after it, when for no reason I got scared. I grabbed the pencil and wiggled out, carrying a big dust ball along with me. I shook it off and backed out of my room quickly.

Mama was waiting at the bottom of the steps. "Come on now, Sara."

"Mama," I said as we walked along in the sunshine. "Can we clean under my bed?"

She gave me a quizzical look. "Is it dirty under there?"

"Dust," I said.

"I didn't know you cared about a little dust, Sara, but yes, I'll give you the vacuum when we get home."

It wasn't the dust that scared me. It was what might hide in the dust. Papa would understand, wouldn't he? Or would he even remember? Would he remember the monsters in the dust and the soldiers on the steps? And even if he did, should I ask him about them? If I asked, would he block the light at the windows again?

"Let's look for new school clothes today. Would you like that?" Mama asked. "You've grown so tall over the summer."

I gave her a smile and she smiled back. It made me realize how long it had been since I had seen her smile so naturally. I knew it was because Papa was working again. I took Mama's hand and we swung our arms back and forth as we walked into the center of town. Lots of my friends had moved to houses in the burgeoning new suburbs, but I was glad we still lived where we could walk into town and I could draw in the park.

"Let's shop for you first, so the groceries won't spoil."

"Ice cream for dessert?" I asked.

She smiled again. "And we'll make hot fudge for it."

She got a big grin back from me as we went into the store. I was about to pick out a skirt and a blouse when Mama put her hand on my arm. "No, Sara, this year we buy from the older-girl clothes."

I followed her past a few younger girls into the older section. Mama picked a dress or two and sent me into the changing room. I slipped into the first one and stood staring into the narrow mirror in front of me. The girl in the reflection was a confused mix of ages. Anklet socks stuck out of grubby, once-white, canvas tennis shoes. A beautiful dress fitted against the thin figure of a twelve-year-old whose hair was coiffed into ragged braids. I pulled at my braids until they loosened and coppery-red strands hung limply around my face. I pushed my bangs away from my forehead. I had always hated having red hair, but right then it didn't seem so bad. I turned around slowly; then faster, faster, so that the flared skirt of the dress flew about my legs.

"And here is another outfit for you to try on," Mama's voice said, as she stuck her arm through the curtain. This outfit was a pair of pedal pushers, matched to a silky blouse with a scooped neck.

I tried it on and marveled again. When I came out in my old clothes, I didn't look any different, but I felt different: older; a little bit new; more like a seventh grader.

"Now for shoes," Mama announced.

I pulled on her arm. "Mama, can we afford all this?"

"Papa's working again on the contract to design the new theatre downtown," she said as if that made everything okay.

She stepped off towards the shoe store and I trailed after her, wondering how it could be that only a day ago Willie Jensen had called my Papa crazy, and today Papa was designing another building and Mama was buying me a whole new wardrobe.

I ran up behind her and called, "But Mama, what if Papa gets sick again?"

She whirled on me and grabbed my shoulders. "He won't!" she said angrily, before she let go and walked on without me.

I stood stock still, riveted to the spot while Mama walked on, never turning back to see if I was with her. I watched her until I had to run to catch up. She was already at the shoe store entrance and there was nothing I could do but to follow in after her.

I waited for her to talk to me again, but she kept all her dialogue directed at the clerk. He brought out thirteen pairs of shoes before I finally found one pair that fit and Mama liked. We left with our bundles, but it wasn't until we were outside of the grocery that Mama spoke to me.

"Sara, you are never, ever to ask Papa about the war, or his family, or let him tell you his stories again!"

My mouth dropped open, but Mama didn't wait for me to answer. She went straight into the market and left me standing outside. I sat down on a bench, my packages piled next to me, but not even my new clothes took the edge off the cold feeling that had lodged itself in my stomach.

One Month, One Year, One Name

School started, and Willie and I were in the same English class, and we didn't get Mr. Yankers. Instead we had a new, young, movie-star gorgeous teacher named Mrs. Trallick. There was a rumor she had been a model before she began teaching. All the boys sat with silly, dazed looks on their faces as she taught, and it didn't matter a bit that she was boring. If one of the girls whispered anything bad about Mrs. Trallick, the boys sneered at her before returning to their dazed expressions.

I didn't wear my new clothes until Mama asked me one day, "Well, Sara, are you going to transform yourself tomorrow? It's picture day. Why don't you wear your new dress?"

"I don't know," I said unenthusiastically.

Papa looked up from where he was reading *The Letters of Frank Lloyd Wright.* "We spent a lot on those clothes. If you do not want them, let me give them to someone who will."

I bit my lip. "No, I want them. I'll wear the dress."

The weather was beginning to get a little colder. Mama came in before I went to bed to offer me one of her baby-soft lamb's wool cardigans to wear the next day if I needed it.

"Sara, what's wrong?" she asked me. "You've been so quiet. Is there a problem at school?'

I couldn't tell her the truth, so I said quickly, "I can barely stand it! All the boys think the new teacher is wonderful 'cause she's pretty, but she's so boring!"

"I see," she said knowingly and hugged me.

The hug made me feel worse because what was really bothering me was that I missed Papa's stories. It wasn't that I wanted him to be sick, or Mama to worry over money. And there were lots of books I could read that had great story lines, but there was something different about Papa's stories.

Late that night I got up for a glass of water, tiptoeing down the steps, carefully skipping the creaky one so I didn't wake Mama or Papa. Everything was indistinct in the dark and I kept bumping things with dull thuds until a strip of light leaked out from under the study door. Could Papa still be up? I opened the door very slowly so I wouldn't startle him if he was in there, but it was only that the lamp on his desk had been left on. I reached to turn it off and knocked a notebook onto the floor. It landed face-up, pages open. Old dates in Papa's handwriting jumped out at me. Papa had printed a list of months and years without days, each entry followed by a name. I pored over the pages before I put the notebook back exactly where I hoped it had been, and hurried from the room. I had recognized some of the names he mentioned when he told me his stories. I forgot my water, crept back upstairs and sat hunched in my bed, hugging my pillow. It came to me, that although Papa probably thought he shouldn't, he believed the stories he told me.

When I woke up the next morning, Papa was in his study. I tapped gently on the door.

"Come in," he said. He looked up. "Yes, Sara?"

"Papa, do you have some extra drawing paper I can take to school with me?"

He went to the flat file behind his desk where he kept paper and commissions he was working on. I glanced quickly to where I had set the notebook, but it was gone.

Papa handed me what I'd asked for, kissed the top of my head, and said, "I'll see you this evening."

I gulped breakfast and hurried out the door in time to catch up with Willie.

"Hi, Sara!"

"Hi, Willie. Did you finish your book report?"

"Yeah. You?"

"Yep. What'd you read?" I asked him.

He was about to answer when dumb old Joe Blacker walked up and pounded Willie on the shoulder. "Come on, Willie, we're gonna play ball before school. Hurry it up, we need your arm."

Willie looked at me and mumbled, "Sorry, Sara."

So I walked to school alone. Amy Parnell came prancing up to me, pushing her budding chest out in front of her, as if that'd make it grow any faster. Her skirts were getting so tight I thought she was going to bust a seam one day, but no such luck yet.

"Are you going to the school dance, Sara?" she asked. She already knew nobody had asked me.

"Nope," I said.

"Well, uh, my cousin is going to be in town, and I thought, well, he needs a date and well, everyone else is ..." She sputtered off without finishing, took a gulp of air and continued, "My mother made me ask if you'd go with him."

I stared at her and I didn't mean to, but I began to laugh.

"Don't laugh at me," she said angrily. "I didn't want to do it!"

"Well, you know what?" I said. Then before I could say tough luck, I found myself saying, "I'll go with your cousin. What time is he gonna pick me up?"

Her mouth was open. "How should I know."

"Well, find out and call my house, okay?"

"Uh, sure, uh, yes, uh…" She practically ran away from me and in that moment, it finally happened. The back seam of her skirt split as she raced off.

That was it! I walked into school trying to keep my laughter in check. I was still smiling in second period and Ellie Peterson glared at me like I was nuts. Every once in a while a stifled giggle would escape me and make Mrs. Trallick look up, until I had to ask to get a drink. In the hall by the drinking fountain, I leaned against the wall until I sobered up. All morning, I watched Amy. The rip kept getting a little bigger. I saw Joe whisper to Mike who whispered to Willie, and I knew that Amy's rip was making the rounds of the class. Suddenly, I was sorry. I saw the boys snicker and I saw Amy look around, trying to figure out what was going on. And I was sorry.

At lunchtime, I tapped her on the shoulder. "Amy, you've got a rip in your skirt."

"What? Where?" she asked, trying to twist around to see.

"I think you should go to the office and call your mom."

She turned very red, put her notebook behind her and sidled down the hall.

"Aw, why'd you go and tell her," Joe said, giving me a shove.

"You know what, Joe Blacker, you're just downright mean," I said, and left.

Willie was waiting for me in the hall. "I'm glad you told her," he said.

"Yeah, me, too."

After school, Willie was waiting for me again. "Can I walk home with you, Sara?"

"Sure," I said. "Who are you going to the dance with?"

"Nobody," he said, kicking at the pavement. "I can't dance. I got two left feet."

"Oh."

"How's your dad?" he asked. "I see him going out again."

"Yeah, he's okay."

"Must feel nice, to have him back to normal."

I heard myself mumble, "Yes." And I meant it, but I still missed the stories. And I missed Papa talking to me in that soft voice he had when the stories were on him.

Nobody was home when I got there. Mama was at her quilting group and Papa was with a client at some site or the other. I sat at the kitchen table with some milk and a sheet of math problems, but I couldn't keep my mind on my work. It was really quiet except for the kitchen clock's *tick, tick, tick*. Willie's words came back to me, and without meaning to, I got up and went into Papa's study. I stood in the middle of the room looking around, wondering why I was there.

Oh, Sara, you know why, a soft voice whispered in my head. I felt my head go up and down in answer.

I opened the doors to a cabinet very quietly. Nothing. Gingerly I pulled out each drawer of the flat file. Only clean sheets of paper and drawings. I jumped, looking around, sure someone would hear me, even though nobody else was home. Nothing in his desk drawers, nothing under the pads I carefully lifted and laid back in the drawers where they nested. Nothing! I ran my fingers over the rows of books on skyscrapers and bridges and world monuments that lined the bookshelves, but the notebook wasn't there either. I was about to give up when I noticed the cushion on his chair was cockeyed. There was the notebook, perched in a hollow hidey underneath the seat. I glanced over my shoulder, plucked it out, put the cushion back, ran upstairs, and bounced onto my bed, clutching the notebook. My hands shook as I opened it. The list was long, but that was all it was. Just a list. I pulled out some paper from my school bag and copied it. One month, one year, one name on each line. When I was finished, I hid the papers under my books, and hugging the notebook, hurried back downstairs into Papa's study. Just as I left the room, I heard the front door open, and there was Papa.

The sunlight caught the blue of his eyes, and I thought for sure that somehow he knew what I had done. My heart was pounding, and then he said, "Sara, could you get me some water and aspirin from the bathroom?"

"Sure, Papa, don't you feel well?"

"Headache," he said. "I'll be in my study. I've work to do."

I closed the bathroom door behind me because my heart was beating so loudly I was sure Papa would hear it all the way downstairs. He had almost caught me! I shouldn't have done it, but I was desperate. I missed his stories so much. So much! I brushed away the tears in the corners of my eyes and poured two aspirin into my palm. By the time I brought them and the water to him, he had his papers spread across his desk.

I bit my lip and asked, "Papa, do you have any good books I could read?"

"I thought you were in the middle of one."

"It's boring," I said. "Everything seems boring now."

"And why is that, Sara?" he asked me without looking up.

"Because I miss your stories," I blurted out. "Real bad! I miss hearing them real, real bad!"

He didn't move his head, but he raised his eyes. "Come here, Sara," he said.

I edged forward and stopped about a foot from him.

"Sara, I can't tell you the stories any more. You understand why, don't you?"

I looked down at my feet.

When I looked up, his eyes were fixed on me. "Don't ask me to do that, Sara. I mustn't." I felt the tears coming and backed out of the room right into Mama.

"To your room, now, Sara!" she said, her face the angriest I had ever seen it. She looked at Papa. He smiled weakly and then bent his head back to his tasks.

I waited nervously until I heard her footfalls on the stairs.

Thrumppp, a voice said. *Thrump.*

"Sara!" Mama said, bursting into my room, "you won't go outside for the rest of the month except to go to school. And if you ever ask your father about his stories again, I will give you a whipping! I have never done that, but I will, Sara, I will!"

I was sobbing, but she turned away. "Mama, I'm sorry!"

"Yes?"

I couldn't answer her because I heard the voice say, *But you love his stories.*

"Stay in here until it's time for supper. Then you can come down, but only to eat. Never again, Sara!" she said with her back to me the whole time. "Never!"

Thrumpppp!

Of course, since I was grounded I didn't get to go to the dance with Amy's cousin. Mama fidgeted the whole day of the dance, and whenever I looked at Papa, he was staring at me sadly, but I was secretly relieved not to have to go. At suppertime, they went next door to Willie's house for a dinner party, and left me alone with a sandwich and a bowl of soup waiting in the kitchen.

As soon as they were gone, I pulled out my copy of Papa's list for the first time since I had made it. I ran my finger down the page. *Constructeur de Maisons* sprang out at me. The castle builder? And there, *Bug Eyes*. When had Papa told me about him? How long ago? Despite all the stories Papa had told me when he was sick, there were many names on the list of which I had no memory at all. I got out another sheet of paper and wrote *Constructeur* at the top. I put the tip of the pencil on the page and then lifted it back up. What did I want to know? I bit the eraser and finally wrote, *Where did he get the enamel for his fingernails?*

I stopped and took up another sheet of paper. *The Poster Boy* went at the top of this sheet. First question: *What poster was he on?*

I scanned Papa's list and saw *Lovely Lili*. She was one of my favorites. Papa said she had been very shy and had rarely spoken to him, but that when she did, she had spoken in distant whispers. I put the pencil down and lay on my bed with my arm over my eyes. Where was Lovely Lili now? Papa had said she was very brave and had saved his life once, but he never told me how. I hopped up and wrote: *How did Lovely Lili save Papa's life?* I heard the front door open and jumped a mile.

Mama called up the stairs, "Sara, Mrs. Jensen sent you a piece of cake."

"Okay," I called, "I'll be down in a minute." I gathered the papers in a disorderly pile and stuffed them under my pillow, then pulled them out and frantically looked around the room.

"Sara, are you coming?" Mama called up again.

Where could I hide them? I stuffed them back inside my pillow case temporarily and hurried downstairs.

"You never ate! The soup is cold, but eat your sandwich. Then you can have the cake and up to bed," Mama said.

Papa came in the door as I sat down at the table. He kissed Mama on the cheek. They looked happy. Mama even hummed a little song as she put dishes away and tidied up.

I scarfed down the sandwich and the cake and was heading upstairs when Mama added, "I'll come up with you and turn down your bed."

"No, Mama, you don't need to do that!"

"I want to," she said and started for the hall. "I want to talk to you a little."

I squeezed past her and took the steps two at a time, sliding into my room just ahead of her.

"Well, now, what was that all about?"

"Cake," I said. I plopped onto my bed. "Energy!" I added as I hugged my pillow and prayed the papers didn't rattle.

Mama sat at the foot of my bed. "Sara, I may have been a little harsh with you. I think you should be able to go out again."

"Thanks, Mama," I said happily, but at the same instant, guilt stabbed me as the papers rattled a tiny bit inside the pillowcase.

"Okay, well, let's turn down your covers."

"Aw, I'm kinda big for you to do that now," I said, even though I really liked it whenever she did. I just couldn't let her find the list.

"All right then, good night." She bent down, kissed me and left, closing the door gently behind her. "She's growing up," I heard her say to Papa in the hall.

As soon as their door clicked, I jumped up. I needed to hide the list and the only place I could think the pages might be safe was in my notebook, at least until I could find a better place. So I stashed them in the middle, pulled on my nightgown and shut out the light. And then I tossed and turned. Every time I got comfortable I thought about how I was in some way lying to Mama.

Only a little white lie, lily white, I heard the little voice say.

Go away, I said to it. Go away.

Morning came up and the sun poked me in the eyes. I pulled the covers over my head, but it was too late. Saturday or not, I was awake.

Through my window I could see Willie practicing cello in his room. I waved and he waved back. The little kids who lived on the block were already outside screeching and shrieking over some delight. Behind their screeches, I could hear Willie's father industriously raking up the leaves that floated down in a profusion of golds and oranges.

I scrubbed at my hair with my fingers and went downstairs in my nightgown.

"Mama went to the store," Papa called from the living room, where he read the newspaper on Saturdays and Sundays.

"What time is it?" I asked.

"Eight-thirty. She wanted to get there early."

I sat down on the sofa next to Papa, got up my courage and asked, "Why'd you name me Sara?"

"Don't you like your name?"

"It's fine, but you musta had a reason to name me Sara."

"What would you have rather been named?" he asked.

"Lili," I said quickly, then looked at my feet.

"Really, *Lili?*" he asked, without hesitation.

"Yes," I said nervously.

I had hoped my question would jog Papa into talking about the mysterious child named Lili, but when it didn't I wasn't sure what to say next.

"Well, it's a pretty name," I pointed out.

"So is Sara, don't you think?"

"Yes, it is," I agreed. "Can I go see Willie?"

"If you eat some breakfast and get dressed first," he said with a little chuckle.

I was at the foot of the steps when I thought I heard him say, "Sara! *Sara, ma soeur Sara!*"

I looked back, but his face was lost behind his newspaper, so I ran upstairs and flipped open my notebook. My papers were so messy, hanging by one hole and stuffed in at jagged angles, edges bent and ripped, that even I had trouble finding the list. Perhaps it wasn't such a bad hiding place after all. I put another number at the bottom of the last page and scribbled *Sara*. Then I changed, brushed my teeth, ran a comb through my hair and dashed outside.

Willie wasn't in his yard yet, so I kicked at the dirt for a few minutes. When he still didn't come out, I knocked.

"Hello, Sara," Willie's mom said.

"Thanks for the cake," I managed to remember to say. "It was yummy."

"I'm glad you enjoyed it. Were you looking for Willie?"

"Yep."

"Willie," she hollered up towards his room, "Sara is here for you."

Willie's mom was a short dumpling of a woman with a loud brassy voice, but I liked her. She always made me welcome and I had never heard her yell at Willie or seen her frown at him.

"You're lucky," I said as we walked outside and climbed into the tree house. "Your mom never gets mad at you!"

He laughed. "You should see her pout when I don't clean up my room."

"Do you clean under your bed?" I asked him.

"You're kidding, right? Who'd do that? Nobody looks under there."

"That's just the point, Willie. If you never clean under there, how're you gonna know what's lurking in the darkness?"

"Aw, Sara, you're funny," he said and gave me a gentle shove. "We're too old for that baby stuff."

"Yeah?" I let it go. I couldn't very well tell Willie that my Papa's stories about the nightmares under his bed had scared me even though I was twelve.

"You wanna help me rake leaves into big piles for my little cousins to jump in when they come over later?"

"Sure, why not? Willie, could I leave something up here in the tree house?"

"Like what?" he asked, scratching at the haircut his mom had just given him. It was funny looking because Mrs. Jensen always did it around a big, old kitchen bowl, shaving the lower part and leaving the top in a thick disarray of curls.

"A list I'm making, but I don't want my Mama to see it."

"Private, huh?"

I nodded. It was private. And special.

"Sure, bring it with you later and I'll stash it in my safe box."

Willie's safe box was nothing more than a banged-up, tin lunch box with red edges. He kept it in the rafters of his tree house. Of course, all the kids knew it was there, but nobody looked in it anymore because they thought they were too old.

"Come over after lunch," he said as we climbed down.

Our house was very quiet as I came in and yelled out, "Papa, did Mama get home?"

"No, not yet. How's Willie?" he asked, coming into the kitchen. He folded his newspaper and laid it on the table as he sat down.

"He's got one of his mom's haircuts again. You know the ones?"

"Bowl cut?"

"Yeah."

"Once they shaved everyone's heads," he said. "They claimed Jews had lice."

Papa had the most beautiful black hair, all shiny and thick. He wore it long enough to pull back into a short ponytail, and sometimes when I heard other adults talking about its length, I'd smile to myself. I tried to imagine him without his hair, but I couldn't.

"People must have looked funny without hair." He caught me in his stare and I knew instantly I shouldn't have said that. "I'm sorry, Papa," I said, even though I didn't know why. "I'm sorry!"

He took a minute, took a really deep breath and said, "It's okay, Sara. You can't be expected to walk on eggshells all the time. I told your Mama that, you know."

I didn't know what to say, so I stood there.

"Come, Sara, sit by me." He patted a chair next to his. "I will tell you a story."

His voice was soft and suddenly I was scared.

"No, Papa! Mama will be mad. She'll blame me!"

His lips opened, and I stuck the newspaper back in his hands.

He looked at it a few moments and then said, "Sara, what did you think of my list?"

I was about to sip some apple juice, and instead I swallowed wrong and it snorted out my nose.

Papa burst out laughing as I tried to quit coughing.

"Yes, I knew you had found it. What did you think?"

I gulped and had to blow my nose before I was finally able to say, "I had a lot of questions."

"Yes? So do I. Have I told you many stories about all those people?"

"Don't you remember, Papa?"

"I remember them like ghosts, like shadow stories." His voice was distant again. Then he shook his head. "Memory is very tricky, but for your Mama—for your Mama, Sara, I have to try."

He got up and wandered to the kitchen window. His fingers played on the curtains, and for half-a-second he seemed about to pull them over the light, but then his fingers stilled.

"I mustn't remember, must I, Sara?"

His eyes pleaded with me, but all I could think to say was, "I don't know, Papa."

At that moment, Willie banged on the back door. Papa's eyes widened, and then he waved his hand at me. "Go, go, Willie is waiting for you."

"Papa," I started to say, but he cut me off.

"Go, now," he said firmly.

The Crash of a Flying Ship

"What do you want, Willie?" I asked irritably as I stepped outside. I had a feeling that I shouldn't be leaving Papa.

"I thought you wanted to rake with us," he said.

"Yeah, but you said later. I haven't had lunch yet."

"My mom is making lunch for everyone, and if you wanna put something in my safe box, we should do it now."

"Oh, all right. Wait here a minute."

I opened the door slowly. Papa wasn't in the kitchen. I peeked into the hall and around the corner into the living room, but Papa wasn't there either. I hurried to my room and rifled through my notebook for the papers. I couldn't find the last sheet, so I took the other two, tucked them into my pocket and headed back outside.

Mama was opening the front door, her arms full of groceries.

"I'll be at Willie's," I yelled.

"Get your jacket, Sara. There's a little nip in the air," she called back from the hall.

I knew I'd toss the jacket in the tree house and probably forget it, but I didn't want to argue, so I grabbed it as I dashed out.

"Hurry," Willie called down from the tree house. "My cousins are here already." He pointed below to the driveway.

Willie had one of those long drives that curved around to the back of the house into a turnaround. Below us, three plump boys bounced out of a car and trotted right into his house without even knocking. Willie's mom greeted them with enthusiasm and we could hear her offering them milk and cake all the way up in the tree house.

"Good, we've got a few minutes," Willie said.

He pulled down the lunch box and I pulled out the papers.

"That's it?" Willie asked. "Can I see?"

I looked at Willie's outstretched hand. If I wanted to hide these here, I was going to have to trust him. He could come up and read them any old time, anyway, so I handed them over.

It didn't take long for him to go up and down the list several times. "What's so important about this?" he asked, his face puckered up into a Willie expression.

"I copied it from my Papa's list."

"Yeah, so? What's it a list of?"

I didn't want to tell him, but I didn't have much choice. "I think it's a list of Papa's stories," I said.

I thought Willie would laugh, but instead he read the list, more slowly this time.

"What do the dates mean?" he asked.

"I don't know yet."

He puckered his face again and after a long moment said, "They're old dates. They go on for about two years."

"They do?" I snatched them back. I hadn't noticed that.

"Why don't you just ask your dad about them?" he asked.

"Can't. Mama won't let me talk to Papa about the stories anymore, not ever!"

Willie puckered his lips for the third time. "Okay, you can hide them here, but I gotta tell you, it's not the safest place."

"Yeah, that's okay."

We climbed down and went into the garage and pulled out two rakes. I noticed the rake handles didn't tower over our heads like they had last year. "Guess we really did grow," I said.

"I guess." Willie beamed. "So, how tall do you think I'm really gonna get?" Willie's mom was super short and his dad was super tall, so it had always been anyone's guess about how big Willie was going to end up.

"This big," I said quickly, putting my hand down about two feet off the ground.

Willie picked up a handful of golden leaves and tossed them in my face. I grabbed a bunch up and threw them back. The little boys ran screaming from the house. "Leaf fight, leaf fight, leaf fight!"

Soon we were all screaming and tossing leaves and running this way and that in the sunshine. Panting, I stopped and watched the others for a minute. It seemed as if Willie wasn't quite as chubby as he had been, as if his body was stretching right out of pudginess. Someone hit me with some leaves and I ran back into the fray.

Mrs. Jensen broke it up when she came out with peanut-butter-pickle-and-jelly sandwiches, with a side of potato chips.

"Willie," I said, when she left, "does your family always put pickles on peanut-butter-and-jelly?"

"Me, I pick my pickles off and save them for the cat," he said with a big grin, picking his pickle out of the peanut butter and dangling it between his thumb and middle finger.

"For your cat?" I repeated dumbly.

"Nope, not for my cat! For Buffy, the scaredy-cat!"

I hit him and he laughed. We raked again after our sandwiches, and the little kids jumped and hooted until clouds drifted in and grayed out the day. When the first drop of rain hit us, the three little boys ran screeching into the house and Willie and I waved goodbye. I dashed for home.

As soon as I burst through the back door, I knew something was wrong. Mama sat rigidly in a kitchen chair, wiping repeatedly at her eyes. She didn't say hello, she didn't reprimand me for dripping water on her clean floor, she never turned her head at all.

"What? What happened?" I asked. "Where's Papa?"

She pointed to his study. The door was cracked, but no light showed out. I reluctantly peeped in. Papa sat in the dark, the curtains pulled tightly over the windows, without one lamp turned on.

"Papa?" I whispered hoarsely.

"Ah, there you are! I've missed you."

That sounded normal. I took a little breath and said, "Are you okay?"

"Tell *Maman* we are going to play with *Rudi*."

My heart sank. "Who's Rudi?"

"You know, the new boy who just arrived."

"Arrived, Papa? Where?"

He looked at me oddly with his head cocked to one side. "Why, here, in the barn!"

I backed out of the room. "I'll go tell Mama," I said shakily.

I stumbled to where she waited for me. "Mama, you'd better call the doctor!"

"I did, I did!" I could hear desperation in her voice.

"Come, come," Papa called, "*Rudi* is waiting for us!"

I looked up at Mama. "Just until the doctor comes," she said and pushed me gently back towards the study. "Someone should stay with him."

Papa motioned me to him, pulled me close and whispered, "Let's go. *Rudi* waits to meet you."

"No, Papa. He's only a story person. He isn't real!"

"Story! Memory! Is there a difference? Memory is real, is it not?"

I was tongue-tied for a moment. Papa stared at me, waiting. My heart raced frantically until I finally thought of what to say. "Once, maybe once it was real, but that was a long time ago. Now it's just stories, Papa, stories you tell to me!" I was terrified. He acted like people were still under the barn floor, waiting for us.

He giggled. I felt tears come, unsolicited and unwanted, flowing down my cheeks, dripping around my nose. He reached out one finger and caught a tear. Something in the back of his eyes seemed to flicker and he said, "Okay, Sara, then just let me tell you a story, all right? But please, don't cry, *ma chère,* don't cry!"

Without waiting for me to answer, he began. "Nobody has come in two days. It happens once in a while when the farmer who brings me food does not think it safe to come. Muffled sounds of trucks have filtered down to me for what may have been days, or perhaps has been only hours. Time has very little meaning anymore, but finally the trucks stop rumbling by. Still nobody comes. Could the soldiers have killed the farmer? If so, who will know I am beneath the floor under the pig trough in the farmer's barn! I am so scared I almost pee, and I am so hungry my stomach hurts at the same time. The pot they left for me smells worse and worse. I put a board over it and try not to breathe too much."

Papa leaned close to my face as he spoke, and his own breath smelled sour and made me crinkle up my nose.

He pulled back and went on. "I must have dozed off, because the sound of the floor boards being pulled aside startles me. The farmer's red, gnarled hands pass bread and cheese down and a pitcher of milk. I pass him up the pot, and in a few seconds it comes back empty, but an odor still lingers. Do you know, I've never seen his face?"

Papa's fingers passed across his own face in the dim light of his study. The sun was setting and a few stray rays sneaked between the curtains and for just a minute, his face was stained red by the sunset. He held his hands up, and they looked translucent at the fingertips and around the nails as the light struck them.

"So dark!" Papa shook his head and went on with the story. "Just as the hands vanish to reset the floor, *Rudi* slides down into the hole with me. The farmer never tells me when someone new is coming, but at least I am not alone when the floor is pulled into place and I am shut in again.

"*Rudi* is short, but I can't say what color his eyes or hair are, for in the dark he looks gray like everything else. When his hand brushes my arm, it is so very smooth, almost like silk. There is a strange timbre to his voice, something that borders between warble and stutter, poor kid. He is stranded in our country, all alone, so he is hiding in the hole with me."

"How'd he get stranded?" I asked, my curiosity nudged into full swing by the story, despite the nagging fear that I was encouraging my Papa towards insanity.

"When I asked him, he said, 'My flying ship crashed!'" Papa turned his hands palms up as if in apology. "He was so little, he still called an airplane a flying ship. I guessed anti-aircraft guns had hit it. He didn't know exactly, but everyone in his family had been killed in the crash. Everyone but *Rudi* died, the same as with my family and me."

Papa shook his head and his hair spun out and he went on, waving his hand as if to say it wasn't important, but it was to me. It was the first time he had ever mentioned that his family was dead. "We shared the cheese and bread and some milk. He was really hungry and ate up a lot of the food. I didn't care. I wasn't alone anymore. We wrapped up in the blankets that the farmer had dropped down. *Rudi* said it was getting colder outside, and we could tell it that night."

I noticed with some relief that Papa had slipped into telling the story in the past tense, the way he usually did, instead of in the present.

"I was asleep when I heard *Rudi* begin to cry, or at least that's what it sounded like at first, like he was whimpering. But the longer I listened, the more I knew he wasn't crying. He was sliding something back and forth, back and forth, and it was making the sound. He wouldn't tell me what it was. He claimed he was calling someone to come get him. I could not bring myself to tell him his imaginary effort was hopeless. I didn't want to make him truly cry. He was so much younger than I, and I didn't want to scare him. Instead, I asked him to tell me about his home.

"Even in the dark, I caught a glimmer of movement and knew *Rudi* had turned his head to face me. 'It's awful down here,' he said.

"Instead of agreeing, I told him it wasn't so bad. It was, after all, better than being dead, wasn't it?

"He thought I was brave. If only he had known how petrified I was! I asked again if he would tell me about where he was from. And, oh, he made up the most beautiful fantasy about his life. His home sat in a little crater surrounded by rolling hills where at night the light was silver and shooting stars flew through the sky. His family raised greens and silver grains which they only watered in the dark because in the daytime it was so hot the water evaporated into steam before it could soak the plants." Papa smiled slightly. "I remember how wistful his voice was as he wove the story. He was sure his family would come for him, but I knew they wouldn't. I knew his family was as dead as mine and no one was hunting for him except for the relentless soldiers."

I reached up and hugged Papa, but he pushed me away gently and sat down in his chair.

"I'm ashamed to say that the story *Rudi* told made me so lonely that I got mad and yelled at him to stop."

Papa cringed back in the chair in which he sat as if someone had just yelled at him, then shook himself and continued more quickly.

"*Rudi* stayed a week, and every night he rubbed his message sender. It was a plaintive, sad sound he made, but at least he didn't cry. We amused ourselves by telling stories. I told him about my cats and my sisters. He told me that someday we would all live on the moon. How I laughed when he said that as we passed away our lives in a dirt hole beneath a barn floor. The farmer brought us food regularly while *Rudi* was there. The portions weren't big for two, but I was grateful he was feeding us because food was rationed and he probably didn't have much for himself, much less for two boys."

Papa started drumming his fingers on his desk. *Thrump, thrumpp!* That was the sound his fingers beat out: *thrump, thrumpp.*

"One night while we slept, a bright light seeped through the floor boards. I had not seen a light since I had climbed down into the hole. I was terrified and backed up against the wall of the pit trembling, expecting the end. But *Rudi* stood front and center and told me not to be scared. How could I not be scared? The soldiers had found us and there was no escape! We were trapped, just like rats. Then I thought the strangest thing. *At last! It is over. Over!*

"Still trembling, I stepped away from the wall, and the barn floor that hid us began to vibrate and shake. Slowly the whole floor above us rose straight up. Something long and sparkling snaked down into the hole and I saw *Rudi* clearly for the first time. He was mottled slightly green by the strange light, but it couldn't hide how deformed and emaciated his body was. His arms were too long, his stomach was too big and his eyes were deep black pools without pupils. It was no wonder he had made up where he was from! They had tortured him. He was one of their doctors' experiments!

"'Come with us, *Michel*,' he begged me. 'We'll take care of you!'

"But I couldn't move. I kept wondering if we had died. Might this light raise us up out of the earth? Out of this grave? Behind the light I could hear the trucks rumbling, coming and coming! If I left, they would catch me. I was afraid again.

Rudi was little and deformed, but after everything, after all the torture, he still believed in fairy tales and people on the moon. I yelled for him to go before they caught him, before it was too late. He yanked at the rope and it pulled him up and up and up into the sky. The light receded, leaving me staring briefly at stars as I followed his escape with my eyes, and at that moment, oh, how I wished I too had gone, but it was too late! The trucks were very close. I could hear their engines revving at different rates. I heard them outside the barn, the soldiers shouting and calling to each other, and just as I heard them at the barn door, poof, the floor dropped back into place. And it was dark again. Dark and cold and lonely and the pot was stinking and there was not a sign that *Rudi* had ever been there."

Papa sobbed. He slid from the chair seat onto the floor and folded himself up into a cocoon. "I can't stand it! I can't! I want to go with you, *Rudi!* Come back for me, please. I believe! I believe! I can go with you, can't I?"

"Papa, Dr. Latham is on his way. It's gonna be okay," I said and tried to believe it myself.

He peeked between his arms, which he had drawn over his head, and said, "I believe." But he wouldn't stand up, and I couldn't get him back into the chair, and all of a sudden I had to get out of the dark room where my papa believed that something from so long ago was still happening.

Dr. Latham sent his assistant, who gave Papa a prescription for a tranquilizer and told Mama to bring him to the office on Monday. Mama stood in the doorway with the slip of paper in her hand looking stunned, but her expression quickly shifted, first to dissatisfaction and then to anger.

"We needed help now!" she protested, wadding the paper up and throwing it on the floor. She stood there, then slowly reached down, straightened the slip out and numbly held it in the palm of her hand.

"I'll go get it," I said.

"No, I'll ask Willie's mother to do it. I'll need your help to get Papa up to bed."

She went to make the phone call to Mrs. Jensen, and left me alone outside of Papa's study. I stared at the closed door, fidgeting from one foot to the other.

Go in, the voice said.

"No!" I muttered and leaned against the wall. "I'm waiting for Mama."

Mama found me sitting on the stairs. She took my hand and together we slipped into the study. Papa sat at his desk, a large sheet of paper laid out in front of him. He looked up as we came in and smiled meekly.

"Would one of you mind turning on the lights? I'm going to work for a while."

Mama and I flashed looks at each other, as I flicked on first the overhead and then lamp after lamp until the room was flooded with light. Papa hesitated, then flipped the switch on his desk lamp so that the sheet of paper glowed brightly.

"Michel, would you like dinner?" Mama asked a bit timidly.

"That would be nice, Lea. I'm a little hungry," he replied.

I was left with Papa. He rolled a pencil between his fingers and finally put it to paper. Without looking up, he asked, "Would you like a sheet and some drawing pencils, Sara?"

"Sure."

He cut a piece from a roll of paper leaning in the corner and handed me a drawing board. While I set up, he reached into his desk drawer and drew out a box, so polished it looked soft where it lay in his hands. Inlaid in brass letters on the top was a name: *Eugène*.

"*Eugène* gave me this after the war," Papa announced, rubbing it between his hands. "His father had been a maker of fine furniture and had made it for him. He gave it to me because I was going to be an architect." Papa ran his hand over the edges of the box and extended it to me. "Here, it's yours now."

"Thank you, Papa," I managed to mumble.

"Open it."

Cradled inside was a set of sharply pointed, graphite pencils in every hardness available.

Papa was watching my face. "I bought them for you. Now draw. Have some fun!"

It was hard to believe this was the same man of only a couple of hours ago.

I was trembling as I sat down to draw, but each time I took out a pencil, I got a little calmer, and with each line I drew, I pondered who Eugene might have been.

Mama came in to tell us that the dinner was baking, then flitted back into the kitchen.

I got up and went to Papa's side. "What project is that for?"

"One I've been working on for a long time. This piece of it is for an observatory. See, here, this section is a deck where you can sit and look up at the stars. There will be benches and chaise lounges there, where you can rest and just stare up and up and up."

"Neat," I said admiringly.

"And here, see this window that runs down from under the roof, turns the corner and runs across the adjacent wall?"

"So you can see more of the sky?" I asked.

His lips turned up slightly. The rendering was delicate, precise, beautiful.

"And what are you drawing?" he asked me.

"Just a person, but it isn't very good."

"Is it someone special, Sara?"

"No, not yet." I had barely placed the shape of the head on the page.

"Do you remember that game we used to play? I describe someone and you draw the person I describe. Okay?"

"I remember!" I exclaimed. "Sure, Papa, go ahead!"

He closed his eyes and began to speak. "A boy, maybe seventeen. He has a scant dusting of dirty-blonde hair, just barely covering his head as it grows back from when he was shaven bald. His eyes are deep set, his face is long and thin, and he has

47

a little mermaid tattooed on the edge of his jaw, so when he speaks or chews, she wiggles and dances."

I was already busily drawing by the time he turned his attention back to his observatory.

"Papa?"

"Yes, Sara?" he mumbled as he drew.

"Where's the observatory going to be built?"

"On a mountain, of course." He touched the paper gently.

"Who's the client?"

"No one," he said. Then after a long pause, he added, "No one you know."

He worked until I heard Mama open the front door. It must have been Mrs. Jensen with the prescription. The door closed. I vaguely heard Mama moving about, and then she called, "Time to eat!"

The table was set with a fresh cloth. Water sparkled in our best crystal glasses. Glazed carrots and mushrooms were nestled in rings around Chicken Marsala. Potatoes sprinkled with a red salting of paprika formed an outer ring around the edge of the plates. Pink linen napkins waited under shining forks, and next to Papa's place sat a bottle of pills. Something sank in me as we sat down. As I nibbled, I watched Papa's hand, waiting for it to reach for the bottle.

His fingers picked up the fork, the knife. The napkin dabbed at his lips. He laughed and chatted with Mama and all the while, the bottle waited.

Mama went and came back with chocolate cookies and bowls of ice cream. Papa licked his lips as he ate, enjoying each taste. Ice cream was one of his favorite treats. Finally he wiped his mouth with his napkin and pushed back from the table, back from the pink tablecloth and the coffee cups and the sparkling water glasses. The bottle sat by his place.

"Clear the table, please, Sara," Mama said.

I rushed from place to place, stacking empty plates, then bowls. Rushing to the kitchen, back I came. I reached for Papa's glass and he reached out and stopped my hand. I picked up Mama's glass and mine and walked slowly into the kitchen. Papa had the bottle in his palm.

"He doesn't need it now," I cried out. "Don't, Papa! Please!"

Mama opened her lips, but Papa spoke first. "Sara, I can't do this alone."

"It's late. Go to bed, Sara," Mama said firmly.

I hesitated and then headed to the stairs.

"Oh, Sara," Papa called after me, "tomorrow we can draw together."

"Sure, Papa," I said in such a low voice he probably didn't hear me. "I'll help you, Papa," I whispered. I glanced over my shoulder and raced up the stairs, raced away from the pills in his hand, from the celebration of something I already hated.

My eyes popped open at six in the morning, the vision of the
face Papa had described still vividly hanging before me. I sat up
and put my feet on the cold floor, padded down the hall, made a
short stop in the bathroom and went straight away down to Papa's
study. Our drawings lay where we had left them. I sat on the floor
with the drawing board in my lap and opened the pencil box. By
the time I heard Mama tread across the floor upstairs, the portrait was close to finished. It was almost eight-thirty and I was
suddenly starving.

"Sara?" Mama called out.

"In Papa's study," I answered.

"What are you doing in here?"

"Drawing, Mama. Is Papa awake? I wanna show him."

Mama stared at my paper where it lay. "It's wonderful, Sara,"
she said in a hushed voice. "So beautiful! Papa will be very pleased
when he wakes."

"He's still asleep?"

"The pills, I guess." She audibly sighed.

I had forgotten about them, maybe on purpose. Mama
wiped at her cheek as she turned away from me.

"Mama," I said, jumping up, hoping to distract her. "Look
at Papa's fabulous design."

She came over to his desk and I heard her breathe in with
a rasp. "What is this?"

"It's an observatory for a client!"

"What client?" Mama asked. "Sara, what client?"

"I don't know. Mama, what's wrong? It's beautiful!"

She didn't speak, but I saw her diaphragm heaving up and down. At last, she managed to say, "Yes, very beautiful."

I don't know why, but it dawned on me. "He doesn't have a client for it?"

"Not that I know of, Sara, but perhaps he does. And even if not, perhaps he just dreams of building it? It is lovely."

We stood over the plans until Mama said, "Sara, scoop up your drawing and take it up to show your Papa. It's time to wake him anyway."

I lifted it carefully at two corners and carried it upstairs, tapped on the door and waited until Papa told me to come in. He was sitting on the bed with his feet dangling over the edge.

"Look, Papa," I said proudly.

He looked and his face folded up and he wept. In that moment I knew I hated those pills.

"Papa, don't cry. Why are you crying?" I said, wanting to hug him, afraid to touch him.

"*Eugène!*" He sobbed the name out.

I looked at my drawing. Eugene? Was this Eugene?

"I knew you could draw him," Papa said.

My mouth was dry and I stood there dumbly. Finally I spread the drawing on the floor and walked over to Papa. His eyes stayed fixed on my drawing as I climbed onto the bed and gingerly put my arm around him.

"Papa, I drew it for you. Please don't be sad."

He patted my back. "I'll be down in a few minutes, Sara."

I hopped down, took the drawing with me and went back to the study. I searched around and finally taped it to a wall Papa faced when he worked at his desk. I stood back to view what I had drawn. The eyes were dark and intense. The little tattoo sat intricately drawn on the jaw. It had made Papa cry. Could it really look that much like a man I had never met? I went into the kitchen and munched on a piece of toast while Mama puttered about in the big stainless steel sink. The smell of coffee and fresh squeezed oranges filled the kitchen.

"Mama, did you ever meet someone named Eugene?"

"No, but Papa wrote for a while to a man named Eugene. Eugene Simmon, I think." She pronounced it in English—not *Eugène* like Papa said.

"Really? There really was a Eugene?"

"Yes, really. Another survivor," she said, and cut through an apple at that moment, slicing it in half.

"Do you know what Eugene means?" I asked. "I looked it up last night." I always looked up the meanings of names. "It means born lucky."

Mama sat down next to me with a cup of coffee and a slice of apple in her hand. "I doubt the survivors of the war felt born lucky." She bit into the ivory slice and a drop of juice dripped over her lip. She wiped at it.

"But they survived! They must have felt lucky."

"I don't know, Sara. Maybe, in a way, but how does it feel to be the only ones left?"

I was still musing over that when she spoke again.

"Papa and I had just married when the first letter came from Eugene. The envelope was covered in beautiful designs and tiny little drawings. Papa cried out in delight as he opened it very carefully, so as not to rip one bit of the exquisite envelope. Inside was a sheet of paper, folded many times. The square of each fold held a drawing, each detailed beyond anything I could have imagined. Papa chortled as he looked at those drawings, commenting and pointing out little things to me.

"'Look here, Lea!' he'd say and tell me stories from the pictures. There were no real words, but every letter from Eugene told many stories!"

"How many letters did Papa get?"

"He got one a month for a whole year. He answered every one within a day, although he rarely wrote letters. He made drawings of buildings to send back and wrote names by each one. One for this friend, one for that, he once told me. One for him, one for her. I wish I had copies. I wish I could remember who they were for." She stopped.

I couldn't remember ever seeing Papa write a letter. I had supposed no one wrote him and so he wrote to no one. He dictated all his letters to Mama, who typed them. The only place I could recall him writing was on his architectural plans.

Mama spoke. "The last month a letter came from Eugene, it was different. It was a thin sheet of paper stuck into an ugly brown envelope, addressed in a different hand. The minute Papa saw it his hands shook. He tore the seal and pulled out the paper. A single image covered the whole sheet. It was a face, completely made up of tiny tattoo-like drawings, with only the eyes, the deep dark eyes, still human.

"Papa cried and cried, and I couldn't console him. Then he grabbed the drawing and tore it and tore it and tore it until the face that had been on it was shredded into bits and pieces. Ripping, ripping! Furiously! His face was crushed and red, his nose dripped!"

"Why, Mama?" I asked, frightened just by the description of that moment.

"All he ever said was that Eugene had finished himself. I was sure he meant he was dead. 'Don't touch that trash, Lea,' he said, and pointed at the bits of paper. Then in the middle of the night, I found him on his hands and knees trying to Scotch tape the scraps back together, but it was hopeless."

We heard Papa on the stairs and Mama stood up so abruptly she rocked the table. He was dressed casually, but neatly. His shirttails were tucked in, his hair was brushed and his face was smooth shaven.

"Did you take your pill?" Mama asked firmly, but I noticed a tremor in her voice.

"Yes," he answered distantly, but as he sat down to breakfast, he smiled happily at me. "So, Sara, shall we draw together again?"

"Sure, Papa." Papa didn't seem too different. Maybe the pills weren't so bad.

"Come, then."

He took his coffee with him and closed the door to the study behind us. He stopped as he saw my drawing hanging on the wall. He walked up close until he was eye to eye with it and simply stood there.

"Papa, why did you tear up the drawing of Eugene?"

He stepped back from my drawing, but instead of answering my question, he said, "I still have the pieces."

A shudder ran the length of his body before he calmly added, "Today the person for you to draw is perhaps seven or maybe eight. She is very pale, her hair so blonde it is almost white. She loves the silver light of the first sliver of a new moon. Her hands are delicate, her eyes are endless pools of watery blue and she always carries a little, brown teddy bear."

"And the shape of her face, Papa?"

"Round, except for her chin which is ever so slightly sharp."

I could see her. "Papa, you're so good with words, you should write."

"No, no, not me. I don't write."

"You used to write Eugene."

He put his face up to mine and almost hissed. "Mama shouldn't have told you. *Eugène* is gone. Gone and finished."

I tasted the salt from a tear at the edge of my lip before I knew I had shed it.

Papa drew back and immediately said, "I'm so sorry, Sara."

"What happened to Eugene?" I asked.

"He was already dead when I got the drawing."

"How do you know that, Papa?"

"His work was done; he was complete. There was nothing left for him to live for. In the corner of the picture, in tiny letters he had written, '*Adieu, Michel. C'est finis.*'"

Papa stopped speaking and a silent spot grew in the room. I prayed the pills would keep him with me. If he left us now, it would be my fault. I wanted to say something to anchor him, to stop him from wandering away, but before I could, his voice got soft as if it came from far away and, out of the blue, he began a story that seemed to have no connection to our conversation.

"That day started like any other for me, shivery-cold and gray. Suddenly the barn floor above me slid away and a stream of daylight fell into the hole. I could see little in the sudden change. All I knew was, I could feel warm air above me. I quivered, expecting the soldiers to shoot me dead on the spot, and just leave me there. They wouldn't have to bury me. They would need only to pull the floor back over the hole and I would be forgotten. But I didn't care. It was too hard to care anymore.

"As I waited for the shots, I lifted my head even though I could not see, but there was nothing. No little pop-pop sound. No burning pain. Instead I heard something drop down the side of the hole and then a woman's voice said, 'Climb out, you little fool!'

"But I was immobilized, still waiting dutifully to be shot. I stood in the middle of the hole, blind and unmoving, my arms spread wide, the perfect target. Still no shots.

"'Suit yourself, then. Raving mad, aren't you? I always told him! Always! But he gave up everything to hide you, you little monster!' Then she spit on me and her aim was excellent. It caught me on the cheek even from that distance. 'It's over, you idiot! The war! It's over!' she yelled. 'Do you understand?'

"When still I did not answer, she spit again. 'I told him to turn you in, but he wouldn't listen. And now it's all over and you will not even come out of there. Well, he made me promise to let you out and now I have. Do you hear? Do you understand anything at all? It's over and if you ever quit cowering like a dog, you can get yourself out of that hole. I'm not coming down for you! I've done what I promised.'

"Of course, the louder she screamed at me, the more immobilized I became," Papa said shakily.

I shivered at the image. Papa, after two long years, standing blind as a mole and this woman leering down at him, screeching at him, more enemy than friend.

"Then she was gone and still, I didn't move, but I listened while my eyes adjusted as someone grunted and dragged things across the ground. I heard a rattle-trap motor turn over and shift into gear, and then unearthly quiet reigned. When I regained blurry vision, I saw that a ladder stood against the wall. I reached out and felt for it with fingertips that had held little other than water and bread for two years. The only things I owned were a teddy bear and a tattered brown bag filled with assorted objects and mementos of my ordeal. I grabbed these scant belongings, stumbled up the rungs, pulled myself out of the hole and tottered towards the door to the barn."

Papa hung his head. "The sun was so bright that I was blinded again, but I stood in its warmth and spread my arms and turned round and round until I stumbled and fell down. Other than those of my feeble movements, there were no sounds.

No trucks, no pigs, no chickens, no human voices. I tried to open my eyes, but had to close them again. Finally I could see a little bit and then a little more and a little more. Dust got caught on my tongue, but my mouth was too dry and cracked to spit it out. The farmhouse door stood wide, dressed bleakly in peeling paint. I made my way towards it and tried to call inside, but my voice barely croaked out of my throat. So there I stood, your age, half-starved, caked with the accumulated fear of two years with no one visible anywhere. My knees wobbled and I had to grab for a porch post to stay on my feet. When the dizziness passed, I peeped around the door and into the house. It was stripped of every stick of furniture. Not a pot or a pan was left hanging on the wall or sitting in the sink. Not a loaf of bread, not a carrot nor a single turnip. Nothing. It was stripped, more naked than a peeled banana."

Papa's comparison made me giggle nervously, but when I saw the look on his face, my smile evaporated.

"The door to the bedroom stood wide and I innocently walked through it, but death occupied that room. Laid out on a bed was the corpse of the farmer. I knew him from the worn hands crossed over his chest. Flies were already settling on his face. I tried to scream, but my voice was too long out of use and nothing came out but a gurgle. I wanted to run, but I was drawn to him. I had never seen his face. As I eased up to his body the flies scattered. His nose was large, his lips broad, his hair white with age. All color had drained from his body except for that in his coarse, red hands. Dead, but still waiting for me. I leaned over and kissed his death-pale cheek. Surely he would awaken from my kiss."

"Like a Sleeping Beauty?" I murmured.

"Yes, that is what I thought, but his cheek was icy cold and suddenly I felt death's fingers clutching at my arms, brushing my eyes, my lips, my nostrils. I dashed from that room, from that empty house, across the yard, across the fields, as far as I could run before I fell sobbing and panting to the ground under the branches of a big tree, still clutching Bear and my brown paper sack. How I got that far I will never know, but who should drop down out of the tree's twisted limbs but *Eugène*."

The look on Papa's face changed and suddenly it was lit with a grin.

"I looked up his name, Papa. You know what Eugene means?"

"No, what does it mean, Sara?"

"Born lucky, Papa. Was he?"

"Yes and no," he said. "What does *Michel* mean?"

"Who is like God," I said.

"Oh! *Eugène* would have liked that. He always said, he was the lucky one and I was the godly one."

"Why, Papa?"

"Let me tell you the rest of the story," he said, ignoring my question. Papa was very good at not acknowledging the questions he didn't wish to answer.

"Do you know what *Eugène* had in his arms? Bright green, under-ripe apples, Sara! The tree was an old apple tree. We gorged ourselves shamelessly until we threw up and after that

Eugène laughed. He was probably seventeen then and very smart. He had yet to speak and it was a long time before I knew he couldn't. He could read and write and that was how he told me things, at least at first. But one day he decided, for no good reason, never to write again. Never."

"So his letters were all pictures?"

Papa laughed and nodded to himself. "Yes, just so." He got a faraway look in his eyes, put his finger to his lips and said, "No more!" He pulled his chair up to his desk and began to draw.

"Papa, that's not fair! What happened? Who was Eugene?"

"It's time to draw now, Sara. Take some paper from the drawer."

Papa wasn't going to tell me any more, so there was nothing for it but to draw. At least I hadn't lost him to the past. I spread a large sheet out and taped it to the edge of the drawing board so it would lay flat. Would this girl also turn out to be someone he had known? Hopefully someone still alive whom I could meet. I tried the drawing from the side, but the face didn't look round enough. I turned the sheet over, laid it width-wise and started again. Delicate strokes in the lightest leads, every hair visible in wispy fine lines. The face I shaded, leaving out any lines except for the sharp little chin. I gave her slightly cupped hands, held out as if offering something invisible to someone. I filled her dress in with flowers in a heavier pattern and then I worked on the eyes. They were hard.

"Papa, do you have a blue pencil?"

He reached into his desk drawer and handed me a lovely pencil with a thick body.

"Be good to it," he said, his eyes never leaving his own work.

I stood up and stretched. Working on the floor made me a little stiff. "Papa, who's the observatory for?"

"Why?"

"I dunno. I just wondered."

He set his lips, then asked, "Is your drawing finished?"

"No, not quite."

"Well, go play for a while. Go play!"

"Papa, let's go for a walk."

"Later, Sara. I want to work while I have the inspiration."

When Papa said that, I knew it was hopeless. He had little sense of weekends, and his work and play often blended into one. He loved what he did. It made him happy. I kissed his cheek and closed the door softly behind me.

Mama was dozing in the armchair in the living room. It was my favorite room in our house, for here the sun poured in and described a bright shadow-copy of the window on the floor. The edges of the sun-reflected window nipped at Mama's feet as she slept. I got a pad of paper and a pencil from my room and began to draw her. She had straight features and a finely chiseled mouth. Her hair was short and curly and her head was tilted and resting on the wing of the chair. I worked for an hour before her eyes fluttered open.

I closed the pad and said, "I'm going over to Willie's, okay?"

She stretched, pulling her arms over her head and arching her neck. Papa called her his *swan* and I could see why.

"Not so fast, Sara. Can I see your drawing?"

I blushed, but opened the pad for her to see.

Mama's eyes blinked quickly and then again. "Oh, Sara, this is absolutely beautiful!"

"It's you," I said.

"Yes? Me!" She reached up and hugged me. "You are your father's child," she said proudly. "Now go. Go! Maybe Willie will pose for you."

Fat chance of that, not that boy, the voice whispered as I left.

"Hey, Willie, wanna do homework together up in your tree house?" I asked when he came to his door.

"Anything to get away from Harriet! Give me a minute."

Willie's sixteen-year-old sister Harriet was pretty in a cheerleader-kind-of-way, but she was really stuck on herself, too, and she truly seemed to hate Willie. Chubby little Willie! She made sure he knew he was an embarrassing thorn in her side every chance she got.

She saw me waiting in the hall and sang out, "You and Willie going up to his tree house?"

"Yep, that's right," I said and smiled sweetly.

She glared at me. "And what will you be doing up there? Something I should tell my mother about?"

She wanted to irritate me, but I just said, "Sure, if you want to," and smiled again.

Now she really glared at me.

"Come on, Sara," Willie said nervously. "Bye, Harriet."

When we got up into the tree house, he asked, "You finished your math yet?"

"Nope."

We spread a blanket on the floor to make it a little cozier and sat down. Willie poured hot chocolate from a thermos into two plastic mugs.

"It's gonna be too cold to be up here soon," he said.

"Yeah," I agreed and looked out over the neighborhood. I liked it up here. It made me feel as if I was high in a tower surveying the world. But today, the cold made me think of Papa buried in the hole, freezing and lonely. I pulled down the safe box. "I gotta add a name to my list," I said. I wrote *Eugene,* without a month or a year to go with it.

We worked on our math problems and by the time we finished them, we were too cold to stay outside any longer. We gathered everything up and retreated into Willie's kitchen. As soon as we got inside, I could hear Harriet chit-chatting to her friends on the phone.

"Promise me you won't ever get like that," Willie said, tossing his head in the direction of his sister's voice.

"Not a chance, Willie."

We could tell Harriet was talking to a boy now, because her voice was all oozy, asking him what he was going to major in when he went to college in the fall.

"What're you gonna be when you grow up, Willie?" I asked.

"I dunno. I wanna be a cellist, but my dad says I can't earn a living being a musician. He wants me to be an engineer."

Willie's dad owned a car repair shop. He made really good money, but he always seemed a little shy about what he did and he was determined that both his kids would be college educated.

"What about you, Sara? What do you wanna be?"

"I'm gonna be an artist."

"Can you make money being an artist?" Willie asked.

"I dunno. Some Picassos and Van Goghs sell for a ton of money, so I guess you can," I said.

"Yeah, I guess so. That's good."

"Yeah, but even if I don't make money, I'm going to be an artist. I don't have a choice. I have to be an artist!"

"You could be lots of things, Sara. You're real smart. You could be anything you wanted."

"Maybe, but there isn't anything else I wanna be, Willie. Art talks to me. It's inside of me."

He chewed on his thumb for a minute and then said, "Well if you can be an artist, then I can be a cellist." He clamped his lips together in a determined look.

We settled into answering our reading questions. We had almost finished when Harriet yelled, "Sara, your Mom just called and wants you home for dinner."

"See you tomorrow, Willie," I said.

"Yeah, Willie, she'll see you tomorrow," Harriet teased as I got to the front door. "Willie's got a girlfriend!"

"Aw, sit on it, Harriet," I heard Willie say as he closed the door behind me.

Papa let me in and we had a quiet meal.

"I'm glad Harriet isn't my sister," I announced when dessert was served.

"Uh huh," Mama said. "Is she still teasing Willie?"

"And me, now. She acts like Willie and I are in love!"

"I see," Papa said. "Well, Willie is a nice boy. Can he support you? What are his plans?"

Papa's eyes were laughing and I balled up my napkin and threw it at him. "Oh, Papa!"

He chuckled at me.

"Papa, could someone make a living as a cellist?" I knew Papa wouldn't laugh at the idea.

"Is that your plan?" he asked. "I didn't know you played the cello."

"It's what Willie wants to do. Could he make a living at it? His father says he couldn't."

"If Willie is a very, very fine musician, then he could. What about you? What do you want to be?"

"She is going to be an artist," Mama said, answering for me unexpectedly. "Aren't you, Sara?"

I nodded my head. "Yes."

"Michel, you should see the picture she did of me!" Mama exclaimed.

"Will you show me, Sara?" Papa asked.

I went to get the pad and when I came back, Papa was in his study, so I took it there. He stared at it a long time before he said, "Yes, it is your Mama. So much my swan!" He raised his eyes and I could see he was touched. "Can I put it up?"

"Sure," I said proudly.

He took it from the pad very gently and with two push pins, pinned it right to the wall.

"There!" he said, stepping back. "Now let's have a candy to celebrate. Come along."

"I'll be there in a minute," I said, wanting a moment alone to admire my drawing. As I turned to follow Papa, I glanced at the drawing of Eugene and stopped. I went up close. Pasted above the eyebrow was a yellowing scrap of paper covered in a beautiful if tiny drawing. I shivered and left quickly. I wanted to ask Papa about it, but I didn't know what to ask. *Why did you stick that there?* Or: *Is that one of Eugene's drawings?* Anyway, I knew it was one of the pieces of Eugene's last drawing to Papa, so I didn't ask anything.

Papa handed me a chocolate wrapped around an almond. My favorite!

"Because I am so proud of you, Sara," he said as I popped the candy in my mouth.

He watched me chew and when I was done, he said, "Now, to bed with you. Go."

"Papa, can we draw again when I get home after school tomorrow?"

"We'll see, we'll see. I have a meeting tomorrow."

Mama was frowning where she stood waiting to kiss me good night, and it made me remember that the appointment he had was with the doctor. I was almost asleep when Mama cracked the door and came in.

"Does Papa still need to go to the doctor?" I asked sleepily.

"I wish he didn't, Sara, but you know how it comes and goes. We can't ignore it anymore. Now, to sleep. Don't worry."

She kissed me. As she turned out the light and shut the door, the voice said, *Ignore it? Oh my, no! Never again!*

Poster Boy

Mama left a message in the school office telling me to go home with Willie because the appointment had been delayed and they'd be late.

"Can I just run home and get my pad and pencils?" I asked Willie's mother when we got there.

"Sure, sweetie, just come right on back."

The house was very still and the afternoon sun was all that lit the rooms. Out of the blue, it felt as if time stopped and I was moving in molasses-thickened air. It took forever for me to climb the stairs, to pick up my pad, to descend the staircase, to open the door to the study. *You're scared,* someone whispered to me. I bent down ever so slowly to reach my pencil box; stood back up, inch by inch; turned bit by bit and found myself staring at my drawing of Eugene. Another tattoo had been pasted up, this one over the upper lip.

I began to shake, but even that motion seemed drawn out and lengthened. Why was Papa reconstructing Eugene?

"Hey," Willie yelled into the house, "where are you, Sara?"

The spell was broken. Time retracted into the moment and I bolted from the room.

"I'm ready," I said, quickly handing Willie my pad to carry.

"You left the study door open. I'll get it," he said. Before I could stop him, he reached into the room and grabbed the doorknob. "Wow!" his voice exploded. "Who did these drawings?"

"Which ones?" I asked, but I knew he was staring at my portraits. "Oh, those! Me. But if you wanna see something super cool, look here."

I pulled him over to Papa's desk, but the observatory had been replaced by plans for the new theatre.

"Darn it! He put it away," I said.

Willie had already returned his gaze to my drawings.

"These are great, Sara! You're already an artist!"

I blushed. I could feel the redness in my cheeks. "It's not much compared to your cello playing," I said.

"How would you know how well I play?"

"Oh, for heaven's sake, Willie Jensen, it drifts in through my windows all year long!"

He cleared his throat and shifted his feet. "I wish, I wish!"

"Next time I wish on a star, it'll be for you to be a cellist, and then we'll both be wishing, so it will just hafta happen."

He smiled as his cheeks turned pink. "Thanks, Sara."

"Let's go back to your house, Willie," I said.

We didn't say much to each other the rest of the evening. Mama and Papa didn't get home until almost eight o'clock. I saw the car pull up to the house, grabbed my stuff, called goodbye and thanks, and raced home. My parents had barely gotten to the front door when I barreled up and flung myself at them.

"You weren't worried, were you, Sara?" Papa asked as I hugged him.

I backed away and said, "Nah, I just missed you guys."

Papa winked at Mama. "Well, you will be happy to know, I won't be taking any pills."

"That's great!" I cried out and grabbed him again and then turned to Mama and gave her another hug. "Can we draw now, Papa? I'm done with my homework. Can we draw?"

"Let me get inside. Then maybe for half-an-hour or so."

He slipped through the door and Mama said quietly behind me, "Sara, no stories, okay?"

"Sure, Mama. Is that what the doctor said?"

"No stories," she repeated without really answering me.

I dumped my stuff on the couch and ran to find Papa. He was munching on a cookie and offered me one.

"How about a walk instead of drawing tonight? The stars are so bright! Would you mind, Sara?"

I was disappointed, but I said, "That's fine."

"Would you like to invite Willie along?"

"Uh huh, sure!"

We put on our hats and coats, met Willie outside, and the three of us started off down the sidewalks. Soon we came to the empty lot that was always covered in dry weeds. Papa tramped into the thatch, his boots crunching on the brittle stems.

"*Thrump. Thrumppp.*"

I didn't want to hear that, but I couldn't help it. Papa was making the sound under puffs of white breath. Willie heard it and innocently echoed it until I elbowed him.

"Ouch," he said.

"Papa," I called and hurried to catch up to him.

He turned, running backwards, laughing. His hair came loose and blew wildly as he ran. "Come on, run! You have to be fast to catch me."

He did little dance-like steps to turn himself around and stretched out into a run. Papa wasn't particularly tall, but he was fast and he quickly left Willie and me tripping over stones and debris hidden in the grass, while he virtually flew ahead of us as if he had winged feet. Finally he came to a dead halt and flopped over backwards onto the ground. By the time we reached him, he was lying spread-eagled, staring up at the sky. We flopped down next to him, gasping for breath.

"Look up!" he said. "Up."

The stars hung crisply above us, every constellation starkly outlined in the dark sky.

"Now, right there," he pointed, "that is the first constellation that *Eugène* taught me."

"Who's Eugene, Mr. Goldman?" Willie asked.

"An old friend," Papa said calmly. "And there, do you see that one? Orion's belt."

"Mr. Goldman, will you tell us one of your stories?"

I froze. I had promised Mama no stories, and I had meant it, but I hadn't considered that Willie might ask for one.

"Which one, Willie?" Papa asked, acquiescing easily.

"I dunno. One Sara has never heard."

Papa turned his head to me. "So you share all my stories with Willie, Sara?"

"No, she doesn't. That's the problem!" Willie interjected. "She's only told me a few and I want to hear them all!"

"All right then, Willie. I will tell you and Sara a story about a boy who loved the stars.

Willie rolled onto his belly and looked at Papa. "Eugene?"

"No, no, this one is not about *Eugène,* Willie," Papa said. He looked up into the sky and his voice changed and I knew he was traveling back to the barn.

"It was cold and dark where I hid."

"Who were you hiding from, Mr. Goldman?" Willie asked innocently.

I held my breath and waited, but Papa said, "No questions, Willie. I don't answer questions."

At least Papa still knew who we were. I released my own breath in a little ball of white air as Papa began.

"It was always dark, but the cold was getting worse and worse that night. I shivered and tried to wrap up tighter in the blankets, but they were old and thin and didn't help too much. My teeth were chattering loudly when the floor above my head slid over and a boy jumped nimbly down. He was athletic and muscular and his features were clean and perfect, like one of the government's posters for the perfect child. Even his hair was the absolutely perfect color of gold depicted in pictures. In fact, he was surrounded by vague yellow light, the kind a flashlight gives off when you read under the covers and don't think we know about it, Sara." Papa poked me.

"You know everything, don't you?" I asked.

"I would have died to have had a flashlight and a book in that hole. Always read, Willie, Sara! It's a gift. But I had neither of those things, and when this boy came, I was sure that the government had sent him to find me, and now he would tell the soldiers where I hid. So I backed away from him, and for a long time, neither of us said a word. Finally, this golden boy said, 'Well, if you are going to be like that, maybe I'll leave.'

"'Are you hiding or not?' I asked him forthrightly.

"He thought that over for a few minutes it. He bit his perfect red lips and said, 'I don't want them to follow me home and find our mountain, so I'm hiding with you for a while.'

"A ruse, I thought. A made up excuse for sure, but why bother with this strange boy if they already knew where I was? No, perhaps he was really hiding.

"'You see, I leave a glowing trail wherever I go,' he said.

"'You left this trail when you came here? You are bringing them to me!' I cried out at him.

"'No, I'm not!' He told me the sunlight made his golden trail invisible, but at night it glowed. So he only moved in the daylight. That was why he was hiding until the sun rose again. In the morning, when they couldn't follow him, he would leave for his mountain. 'But, I need to rest before I rise again,' he said."

"Wait, let me get this right," Willie interrupted. "This boy left golden trails in the dark, but when the sun rose, they diasppeared?"

Papa didn't answer. He was deep in the story now, and he kept talking as if Willie hadn't spoken.

"'So what shall we do until morning?' the boy asked me, looking around.

"'There is nothing to do down here,' I pointed out to him. The hazy light he gave off illuminated the hole just enough that for the first time I was able to see where I was living. The

73

walls were dirt with a few bricks sticking out here and there. The floor was shiny where I had tramped the dirt hard when I paced and muttered to myself. That was all. It was exactly as I had thought.

"'Let's play a game,' the boy said. 'Lie on your back!'

"I did what he said. He put his feet on the bricks and climbed up the walls, until he was close to the floor boards that served as a ceiling over the hole. He put his finger on them here and there. A touch, a touch, another, another until he climbed down.

"'What do you want me to do?' I asked.

"He told me to wait. He grabbed up a blanket and wrapped himself in it so that he was covered, head to foot, and as he did, the glow he gave off was blanketed out."

Willie laughed. "That's a funny pun," he noted.

The stars were so bright I could see Papa's face and he was smiling. Was it because of Willie or because of something else, somewhere in his mind?

Papa started speaking again. "'Look up,' the blanket-wrapped boy said. I did and there, on the dull boards where he had touched, glowed constellations. They didn't glow in the cold silver that you see up there," Papa said and pointed above us. He paused just the right amount of time for us to take in the silver confetti in the sky. "They burned, like little hot suns. Bright and yellow.

"The boy asked in a muffled voice, 'Well?' But I couldn't speak because I was holding my breath, and in impatience he threw off the blanket. Of course, the stars diminished and then vanished because of the light he gave off.

"I was awed, and when he saw that, he burrowed back out of sight, and the stars came out again. He spent the night telling me stories about the people who inhabited the heavens, and it wasn't until years later when I studied mythology in college that I learned his stories were all wrong. But for that one, cold night, I basked in those tales."

"What happened to the glow-boy?" Willie asked.

"What? Oh," Papa said distantly, "at dawn he left. He climbed the bricks and pushed back the floor. Just before he heaved himself up over the lip of the hole, he asked me, 'Don't you want to come? Come, come up to the mountain with me, *Michel*.'

"I couldn't. I begged him to stay, but he said if he did, the dark would win. He left me there in the cold and I never felt so alone as when I looked at the ceiling and the hot little stars were gone."

Papa stopped. It was so quiet that I jumped when Willie said, "Gee, Mr. Goldman, you tell the best stories! How do you think them up?"

Papa didn't answer and when I looked at him, starlight glinted off a frozen tear on his eyelash.

"Let's go! I'm cold," I said, hopping up.

Papa sat up slowly and got stiffly to his feet. I took his hand. When Willie waved good-bye at his driveway, Papa still hadn't spoken.

"Papa, I won't tell," I promised.

We stood silently in front of the door. I waited for Papa to speak, but he didn't. After a few minutes, Mama threw open the door and said, "You two nitwits are going to freeze! Stop talking and get in here. I've hot cocoa waiting for you."

I held my breath as we unbuttoned our coats, afraid that Mama would notice Papa's silence, but at last he blinked and said, "With marshmallows, Lea?"

"Of course, Michel, come on!"

He blinked again, and a silver drop of liquid fell from his eyelash.

SPRING TIDES

For School

In the spring of seventh grade, we studied family history. For the first assignment we were supposed to go back as far as we could and begin a family tree. That would be easy for Mama's family. Nana had a beautiful tree framed and hanging over the mantel in her house. All I had to do was copy it down. But Papa's family presented a problem. I worried over when the best time to ask him about it would be, practiced what I would say in front of the bathroom mirror, and then waited until we were eating our Sunday dinner to bring it up. My heart started to beat a little faster as I cleared my throat and said exactly what I had decided not to say.

"Papa, I need to know about your family for a school project."

Both Mama and Papa looked totally startled, and Mama actually choked on a bite of mashed potatoes.

Papa looked down at his plate and murmured, "There is no one but me."

I took a deep breath and said desperately, "No, Papa, you have to tell me! Otherwise, I'll get an F."

"I was ten when everyone died." That's all he said before he shoved back from the table and left the room. The door to his study closed behind him.

"I'll write you a note and explain. You won't fail, Sara," Mama said quietly.

"Thanks Mama," I said, but I was disappointed.

Mama patted my hand. "Sara, I'm not sure Papa remembers his family well enough to tell you about them."

"You aren't mad at me for asking, are you, Mama?"

She sighed. "No, Sara, I'm not mad. Go on and talk to him."

He was drawing when I knocked and went into his scantuary, for that was how I was coming to regard it. It was the largest room in the house with two floor-to-ceiling windows surrounded by naturally finished woodwork. The walls were a warm ivory white, and the bookshelves against the walls matched the wood-work and the baseboards. I was allowed access to anything in his study, except for the large walk-in closet right by the doorway to the room. That closet was usually locked and any time I showed interest in it, Papa became agitated and grumpy. I had learned at an early age not even to touch the doorknob.

Papa was perched on a stool, leaning over his drafting table in the corner. He had laid a long, skinny piece of paper width-wise across the table. The house he was designing sat buried in a hill from which rock gardens spilled. I watched his hands fly across the page, adding to the shading, extending the rooms above the first floor. You could look into the rooms through the windows and see artwork hanging on the walls, and the pat-terns of the fabric that covered the furniture. There was no color. There was never color in Papa's drawings.

"Hi, Papa," I said.

His hand stopped moving, but he didn't speak.

"That's beautiful!" I said, pointing at the drawing.

He tenderly brushed his fingers over the surface of the pa-per. "It's for your Mama. Someday I will build it for her."

"Can I live there, too?"

He looked up now. "Of course, Sara. Come, come here. I have put two studios in this house, one for you, one for me."

I moved closer to him and he gave me a guided tour of the whole house.

"Where will you build the house, Papa?"

"I'm still looking for the perfect place," he said. He laughed lightly. "Of course, I may have to design it all over again to fit whatever site I finally decide on."

"Uh huh."

"Sara," he said out of the blue, "I am sorry I cannot help you with your project."

"But Papa, there is no one else to ask!"

"No, Sara, this is a project I cannot help you with."

"You mean you won't help me with it," I corrected him, trying not to be angry.

"I will help you with anything else, except that!"

"Anything else?" I asked. "Okay then, my art teacher, Mr. Paleri, really wants me to put a drawing into the area-wide art competition at our school tomorrow night and I have to bring it in the morning."

"Congratulations, Sara."

"I need help deciding what to enter."

All along the white spaces of Papa's study hung the drawings I had been doing since the fall. Each time I finished a portrait description, Papa tacked it up. And each time he put one up, another little scrap of drawing filled in another space on Eugene's face.

"Which one should I take, Papa?"

He stood slowly, pencils falling from his lap. "You want to take one?

"Uh huh. Would it be all right?"

"But Sara, I..." He stopped in mid-sentence. "Which one?" We let our eyes travel the walls. "Here," Papa said, gently pulling out the push pins. "Here, take her."

"Okay, but what should I title her?"

"You'll get her back, won't you?" he asked.

"Of course."

He rubbed his chin. "Call the drawing *Lovely Lili*." He picked it up carefully and laid it into a black, board portfolio and tied the strings. "Bring her back, promise?"

"I promise," I said solemnly and picked up the portfolio, feeling oddly proud. I carried it into the living room where Mama was reading. "Could you help me fill out this entry form so I can submit one of my drawings in a competition? Your writing is neater than mine."

"Of course. Which picture is it?" she asked as she opened the portfolio. "Oh, she is one of my favorites! Now, let's see the form. Your name, address, grade, phone number, title and sale price. All very professional, Sara."

I nodded.

Mama started writing: Sara Goldman, 45 Leaping Frog Way, Grade 7, *Lovely Lili*. "What price?" she asked.

"Not for sale," I said.

"Not for sale?"

"Papa made me promise."

She wrote it in and laid the pen aside. "Did you ask Papa about his family?"

"There isn't much point, is there? Sometimes I wonder if he is having me draw them for him, one at a time, Mama. Was there anyone named Lili in his family?"

"Not that I know of."

"What were his sisters' names?" I asked with baited breath.

Mama sighed. "He named you after the older one. And I think the little one was Berta, but I'm not sure."

"Do you know what his parents were named?"

She shook her head.

"But no Lili?"

"No, no Lili that I know of. Now, go brush your teeth and I will write you a note for tomorrow about your family tree."

"Mama, what'll you say in the note?"

She looked up over the edge of her glasses and said, "I will say that everyone died in the war; that all records of them were destroyed and that we do not talk of it in our house. Is that okay with you?"

"Yeah, I suppose so." I went upstairs and brushed my teeth and my hair, and then I combed my old snuggly bear's fur a little, turned out the light and slept.

I woke up late, so Mama drove me the seven blocks to school. I hopped out and slammed the car door. Mama waved and I dove into the crowd of kids, mashing through the front door, trying to protect the portfolio that cradled Lovely Lili.

"Watch it," Butch said.

"Keep that thing away from me," Joe Blacker snapped.

I managed to slide through the hall to the art room to deliver *Lovely Lili* to Mr. Paleri without further mishap.

"So, Sara, what did you bring?" He picked up the portfolio and spread it on a table and stopped speaking.

"Don't you like it, Mr. Paleri? I could have brought a different piece!"

"No, no! It's beautiful! Exquisite, Sara!"

"It's weird is what it is," Butch said from behind me.

Mr. Paleri frowned at him and carefully closed the covers of the portfolio over Lili. "What have you brought in for the show, Butch?"

He pulled out a paper thick with paints and plopped it onto the table where my drawing had laid a moment before.

"Now that's something, isn't it, Mr. Paleri?" Butch asked.

"Yes, quite something," Mr. Paleri said. I could see he was trying to keep a straight face.

The bell rang and we all scurried for our stools at the art tables. Amy had her arms wrapped around a clay pot and even Joe Blacker was pulling out a sheet of paper from his notebook that I could see was covered in a cartoon character with a flaming red cape.

"Okay, everybody who has an entry they haven't given me yet, please come up now. No pushing, no shoving. Be sure your entry form is attached to your piece."

I stayed in my seat as kids crowded up to Mr. Paleri.

"Now, for today, you need to write a little description of why you entered the contest and how you did the art you are entering. I'll walk around the class in case any of you need help

83

or have questions. The essay will be displayed right next to the artwork, so be sure you do a good job. I need it by the end of class."

I stared at my paper, trying to think what I could say. I entered because Mr. Paleri had asked me to, but what was I going to say about how I did the drawing?

"Having trouble?" Mr. Paleri asked me as he walked by.

"Well, a little. I don't really know why or how I did my piece."

"Yeah, that's cause she didn't do it at all," Joe said, looking up from across the table.

"Yes, I did!" I said. "It's a portrait, but when I do art I don't always think about why or how while I'm doing it."

"Yeah, sure!" Joe muttered nastily.

Mr. Paleri ignored him and said, "Just write that down, Sara. Who did you draw?"

"My Papa describes people to me and I draw them. It's a game we play," I explained.

"Yeah, right. Your father draws them for you and you copy them," Joe said.

"Be quiet, Joe," Mr. Paleri said. "Sara doesn't need help from anyone. She draws very well."

Mr. Paleri walked on, but Joe stared at me and stuck out the tip of his tongue. "Cheater," he whispered.

I glared at him and he grinned maliciously back at me.

"Mr. Paleri," I called. "Can I move to another table?"

I got up and went to sit in an empty seat next to Amy.

"I like your drawing," she said.

"Thanks. Your pot is nice, too."

I settled in and wrote. I stopped to say good-bye to Lovely Lili as Mr. Paleri hung her in a prime spot.

"See you tonight," he said. "Bring your parents."

The Ghostly Child

It took me a long time to get dressed. It was my first show, and I wanted to feel special. Mama said I could wear my pedal pushers and blouse, so that part was easy, but I fiddled with my hair for a long time without getting it right. I went down to Mama with my brush and she French braided it, and when I looked in the mirror it was perfect. She lent me a silver necklace to wear, so that when I was done, I couldn't help but feel almost pretty and kind of grown-up.

Papa had come home while all this preparation had been going on and had immediately holed-up in his study. I tapped on the door and went in. A smile spread across his face.

"You are so beautiful, my Sara! Are you excited?"

"Nervous!" I stated, then tried to stop myself, but couldn't and burst out with, "Papa, how did Lovely Lili save your life?"

"Sshhh, Sara. No stories. We promised."

"But, Papa, what if someone asks me who she is? I should know, shouldn't I?"

"Sssh, now go out and I'll be there as soon as I put this work away. I've a surprise for you and Mama."

Mama was standing in the hall, folding her lips together to even out the peach-colored lipstick she had just put on. She wore a baby-blue spring suit that set off gold highlights in her curls.

"How do I look, Sara?" she asked, turning around and around for me to see.

"Beautiful, Mama." She was slender and long-legged. A little pearl drop swung at her neck as she turned.

"And you, Sara, you look, well there are no words for how pretty you look."

Papa came out of the study and beamed at us. He helped each of us into our coats, for the evenings were still cool.

"Mama, aren't the stars beautiful?" I asked, leaning back to peer at them as we walked.

"Watch where you're walking, Sara! Just like your father, with your head in the clouds and your thoughts in the heavens."

"Is that so bad, Mama?"

She stopped and then started walking again. "No, Sara, not so bad!"

Papa laughed and we walked along happily until we came to the new restaurant that had just opened the week before on the main street of town.

"Here!" Papa said. "I made us reservations in honor of the night of Sara's first show."

They seated us at a round table in a back corner, lit by a lavender-scented oil lamp. Placed next to it was a glass holding a single purple orchid. My father pulled the chair out for Mama and smoothly slid it in as she sat down, then turned to me, but I was already seated.

"This is lovely, Michel," Mama said.

"I ordered ahead for us."

As I watched Papa, I imagined him as a gallant nobleman. His demeanor was perfect. His hair was tied back, he wore a dark suit with wide lapels and his eyes were alight with romance as he watched Mama. Everything was perfect.

Papa ate with a gusto he never demonstrated at home. I barely noticed what I was eating as I watched my parents. I felt like a princess in a fairy tale. The dessert tray came and I ogled a chocolate crème pie. While the waitress got coffee for my parents, Mama went to the lady's room. She held her shoulders back, head up, and slid between tables as men's eyes turned ever so slightly to follow her.

"So, isn't this nice, Sara?" Papa asked. "Are you having fun?"

"It's beautiful, Papa. Perfect!"

"Yes? Good," he said with a satisfied smile.

The pie was melt-in-your-mouth delicious. Mama tasted it and her tongue circled her lips where only a remnant of the peach color remained. When we left, I copied how she held herself and felt myself slide gracefully between the tables. My Papa was a prince that night, and my Mama was Cinderella, but I couldn't think who I was. The ugly duckling came to mind, which I hoped meant I would make it to *swan*.

Outside, we giggled as Papa tugged on his belt, complaining it was going to break. Mama poked his thin waistline playfully and we giggled some more. When we got to the school, the lights were blazing. Lots of cars filled its small parking lot, while others were parked illegally, but no one seemed to care. I excitedly pulled Mama by the hand down the hall, with Papa following behind. When I looked back, I could see that he was nervously clinging close to the walls. Papa looked like he wanted to bolt from the crowd.

"Come on, Papa, this way," I called.

He hurried up to us and Mama caught his hand in hers. The art room was filled and it was hard to get in. People had come from all over. Parents chattered to each other and teachers worked their way from one group to the next.

"Where is your piece?" Papa asked.

"On the other side of the room," I said.

Papa took the lead and pushed forward through the crowd. We came to a halt in front of Lovely Lili. There she sat, but there was no ribbon next to her. Something else was wrong. Someone had drawn a handlebar mustache on her. I didn't move. Papa didn't move. Mama didn't move.

Around me, a couple of kids hurried by and I saw Butch drag Joe up, pointing in our direction with a muffled laugh. For once even Joe looked uncomfortable.

I felt Mama put her arm around me. I had promised Papa Lili would come home safely, and here she was, mutilated. I looked at his face and it was filled with anger. I couldn't remember ever seeing my father angry before.

"Uh, Sara, Mr. and Mrs. Goldman?"

It was Mr. Paleri.

"I am so very sorry. I don't know how this happened. It was damaged when I came back from lunch."

Papa looked at him and said, "And the ribbon?"

Mr. Paleri couldn't meet Papa's eyes. "I am afraid it didn't win a prize."

"No? And why not?" Papa asked icily.

I noticed that the room was growing quieter. Poor Mr. Paleri stood there absolutely chagrined. "The judges, uh, well, uh, they thought either Sara had copied the drawing or gotten help."

I heard Butch say loudly so I was sure to hear, "See, you were right, Joe!"

Mama and I had our eyes fixed on Papa. His mouth was set in a thin line and when it opened he said clearly, "Were they accusing my daughter of being a liar?"

"No, no! I'm sure they weren't."

Papa didn't answer. He pushed through the people that stood between him and Lovely Lili, and carefully detached my drawing from the wall. "We are going home. Come, Sara, Lea."

"Wait, wait!" Mr. Paleri said, but Papa didn't stop. The crowd parted as we left.

I looked around and saw Butch. He was smiling broadly, enjoying the moment for all it was worth, and I knew, just knew, he was the one who had defaced Lovely Lili. I stared right at him and his smile faded.

"I'll get you," I mouthed at him.

Then we were outside and Mama, in her navy blue spike heels, was scurrying awkwardly after Papa. I ran to catch up.

"Papa, can we erase it?" I asked as I caught his arm.

"No, Sara. It is in ink."

Suddenly, I felt sick. I had let Papa down. I dashed ahead with tears streaming down my face. I ran until I thought my lungs would burst. Papa caught up to me when I stopped, heaving for breath, a stitch in my side, my nose running.

"Sara, Sara!" he said.

"Papa, I let you down. I let them hurt Lovely Lili!"

He put his arm around me and walked with me to the front door. Mama came in a few minutes later and took me up to my room while Papa put Lovely Lili back on the door in his study.

I went in the bathroom, blew my nose, and washed my face, and changed into my pajamas. When I was ready I called to Papa, but he didn't come, so I went to find him. He was in the dark in his study.

"Do you know, Sara, what the most amazing thing was when I climbed from that hole?"

"No, Papa."

"The soldiers were gone and the world was beautiful. Such simple things."

"Yes, Papa. Papa, are you all right?"

"All right? Yes, I suppose so. Are you?"

I bit my lip and said, "No. I'm mad!"

"Yes, mad. That's good! Better than hurt or afraid. Come, let's go into the living room."

We sat together on the sofa and he gently squeezed my hand. Mama called to say goodnight to us from the stairs, but we stayed like that, comforting each other, without speaking for a long time. Finally Papa said, "Do you know how *Lovely Lili* saved me, Sara?"

"No, Papa."

"A story, just this once. It was during the second year of my imprisonment. Two years is a very long time to be locked up, don't you think? Well the farmer came less and less frequently and I was scared. Very scared! I was afraid of being left alone forever, of dying there all alone. And I thought I was growing as mad as a March hare. I talked to myself and I sang myself to sleep just to keep myself company. One day, when I awoke, *Lili* was there. She was very, very small. Very thin and so pale I could almost see her in the dark. She couldn't speak in more than a whisper. She put my fingers on her neck and made me feel the deep rope burns there and there." He stopped and touched my neck. "I gave her a little water, which was all that I had to offer and she thanked me. I asked her what it was like outside and she said in that mere whisper, 'It's winter and the trees are hung with lace. There is ice on the ponds and you can see little fish beneath it.' She stopped between words to sip water. I wished I could see all that. I really did. I actually thought of climbing out into the night. 'But you can't. You might get caught,' she pointed out to me.

"My spirits sank when she said that and I hid my head under my arms. Then I looked up and asked how she had managed to get away and not be caught.

"'Oh, I am a ghostly child. I easily went unnoticed.'"

Papa sighed and his body went rigid.

"But how did she save your life, Papa?"

Another sigh before he managed to say, "Sara, I was dying of loneliness. All alone. So lonely. You cannot imagine. No light to read by, no books to read anyway. No pencil to draw with, no paper to draw on if I had had a pencil. I was alone in the dark except when someone came. But they always left. Always left me alone in the dark."

I patted Papa's hand and said, "It's okay, you don't have to tell me."

"When I was first buried beneath the barn I frequently thought of sneaking out at night, but I never did it. The hole seemed safe and cozy. The longer I stayed, the less able to think of leaving did I become. I was hunted. I knew they were just waiting for me to step out into the night and they would pounce. *Hold your breath. Don't make a sound.* Yes, that was it, what my mother had told me to do. Hold my breath."

I heard him catch his breath and I waited, watching, wondering if he would turn blue, but instead he let it out in a whish.

"*Lili* left me, too, but she gave me something before she left. Her teddy bear to keep me company."

Papa shook off my arm and rose up. "Enough. Enough. To bed."

"Thank you, Papa," I said.

"For what?"

"For sharing Lovely Lili with me."

I went slowly up the stairs.

You let them violate me, the little voice whispered, and I knew who spoke at last. Lovely Lili.

A Gathering of Cellos

Mama came to my bedroom in the middle of the morning to get me up.

"Willie is here for you," she told me.

"Tell him I'm sick, Mama. I don't feel good." I burrowed further into my blankets.

Mama sat on the edge of my bed. "Maybe heartsick, Sara?"

I tugged at my covers and tried to hide my head. "I don't feel good is all. My nose is stuffy."

"Stuffy? Uh hum," she said.

I buried my face in my pillow. After a minute, I heard the door close.

I sniffled. I had spent the morning crying under my covers and now my nose really was stuffy. I reached for a Kleenex, blew, wadded it up and stuffed it under my pillow with a pile of others.

Papa knocked gently on the doorframe and pushed the door open. "So, you are still hiding?"

"I'm not hiding. I'm sick."

He smiled. "Sara, come down, eat breakfast or maybe it's lunch," he said, glancing at his watch.

"Papa," I said, hugging my bear. "Are you mad at me?

"Why? Why would I be mad at you? You didn't draw a mustache on *Lili's* upper lip, did you?"

"No."

"But? What is the *but*, Sara?" he asked me.

"Well, I didn't win anything and she got ruined for nothing and. . ."

"Stop, Sara! You won something. Do you know what?" I shook my head. "You won the disbelief of the judges that you were that good. But you know you really drew that portrait all by yourself, so that must make you an amazing artist, mustn't it?"

I hadn't thought of it that way. I had just felt belittled, but Papa made the insult a compliment.

"Now, stop this. Come down. Live, draw; eat, draw; play, have fun in life; draw!"

"Papa, okay, okay, I get it. I'll be down in a minute."

He pulled Bear from my hands. "So she comforts you, this old bear?"

"Bear is a him," I said.

"No, no, Bear is a she." He gave Bear back to me and started to leave.

"Him," I corrected teasingly once more before he left.

"That isn't what *Lili* told me when she left Bear with me," he said over his shoulder. His footsteps were on the stairs and I was holding Bear an arm's length away from me, staring at him. Or was it *her?* I put Bear down and jumped out of bed in time to hear the front door close.

"Where'd Papa go?" I asked Mama.

"He has a client meeting at a site until late."

"On a Saturday?"

"Yes. Breakfast now?"

"Sure, Mama. Toast and orange juice."

"Okay," she said.

"Mama, there must have been a real Lili, just like there was a real Eugene."

"What? Why would you say that, Sara?"

"Because Papa says Lili gave him Bear."

Mama bit her bottom lip. "I don't think so, Sara."

Mama was wrong. I was sure of it, I sensed it, but I had no way to prove it. "Mama, I'm going to draw this morning. Do you think Papa would mind if I work in his study?"

"Sara, you're going to Willie's concert, remember? His performance is today."

"Oh m'gosh! I forgot." I shoved my toast into my mouth.

"Slowly, slowly. What manners you have! There is still time. When you've finished, put on your pink dress."

I didn't like the pink dress anymore. It made my hair too red and made the rest of me look like a little girl. So I put on the dress Mama had picked for me at the end of the summer and fished out the silver necklace from the night before. I slipped my big, flat feet into my dress shoes, shook my hair loose from its braid and surveyed myself in the mirror. Not too bad.

Mama smiled as I ran out to the Jensen's and when Harriet opened their door, she shut her mouth, at least for a moment before she yelled, "Hey, Willie, your girlfriend's here, looking almost cute."

Willie's face was red when he came down in his suit. He looked nice. His tie was blue like his eyes, and his shirt was bright white and starched.

"Do I look okay?" he asked. "'Cause you're staring at me."

"Uh, you look real handsome, Willie."

"Yeah, well, Harriet was right for once. You look nice, too."

"That's a first, Harriet and us agreeing on anything! Are you nervous?" I asked him.

"No," he said, "but I'm glad you're gonna be there."

He stopped in one of those deadly silences old romance movies always had in them.

"Uh, Sara, I'm sorry about your picture. It was the best thing in the whole dang show."

"Thanks, but I'm gonna get that Butch!"

"You think he did it?" Willie asked.

"Oh yeah! He was smirking away at me. He looked like he could barely keep from whooping!"

"Watcha gonna do?"

"I don't know yet, but don't worry, I'll figure it out."

Willie grinned. "Can I help?"

"Sure, I could use a co-conspirator."

We waited for a while and then the whole Jensen family and I piled into their car. It was a big, beige Caddy with matching leather seats and dark brown trim on the doors. Mr. Jensen proudly pointed out that the cello fit easily into its cavernous trunk.

I got pushed right up against Harriet, whose perfume nearly gagged me. Luckily the ride was short, so the smell didn't make me throw up on her.

"See ya later," Willie said. He picked up his cello and hugged it lovingly as he walked in a side door.

The rest of us went in the main door of the church where the concert was to be held. I glanced down a hallway. Big, black cello cases had been lined up in the hall like a crowd of people waiting to get into a movie theatre. Somebody had set a fedora on one, increasing the effect. I closed my eyes and saw a painting as clear as day.

"Whatcha doing, you little weirdo?" Harriet asked me.

"Memorizing something," I said.

"Weird, weird!" she said and fluffed at her rigidly hairsprayed hairdo.

"Weird," I muttered to myself as I watched her.

We sat in the shiny brown pews. I had never been in a church before. It was pretty with light coming through yellow stained glass windows. The crowd buzzed until the teacher came out. Everyone got quiet and the fifteen cellists trooped out, sat with their cellos between their legs, bows ready, and waited. The program called them a *cello choir* and Willie had two solos. He made his cello sing in a deep tenor. It was a kind of sound I had never heard. Willie looked different with the big instrument balanced between his knees, his head cocked, rhythm infusing all his movements. He wasn't clumsy or chubby when he played the cello. The more I listened, the more clearly I saw the painting in my head, and the more anxious I became to go home and start it.

When it was over, everyone crowded around the musicians while I peered down the hall again, engraving the details of the black cases in my mind's eye. Light poured across the stark red and black tile floor in front of them, contrasting with the old wooden walls. At the far end, a door with a pointed arch above it crowned the hallway.

"Hey," Harriet called, "come on, Sara. My father's ready to get the car."

I hurried after her.

"Willie's just getting his cello," Mrs. Jensen said. "Wasn't it something?"

"Yes, ma'am, it was," I said.

"It was okay," Harriet admitted. "Willie was pretty good."

Willie put his cello in the trunk, slammed it and climbed in next to me.

"So, what'd you think, Sara?"

"He wants to know what Sara thinks! See!" Harriet said knowingly.

"Now, Harriet, leave them alone."

Willie and I stopped talking. I felt dumb, sitting there. Willie looked out the window the whole way home.

As we got out, Mr. Jensen said, "Glad that's over."

I looked at Willie, but he wouldn't meet my eyes.

"Bye, Willie. See you later," I said.

Mama was reading in the living room when I plopped down in a chair and slouched into its cushions.

"You should go change your clothes," she said, without looking up.

"Can we go to the art supply store, Mama? I need paints."

"Sara," Mama said, pointing at herself, "it's me, Mama. I know nothing about buying paints. Wait for Papa."

"He might be too late to go and I need to start this painting," I said insistently.

"Need?" Mama asked, taking off her glasses.

"Yes! Need!" I nodded my head up and down for emphasis.

"All right, but change your clothes first. If Papa isn't back in half an hour, I'll take you. How was the concert?"

"Willie's really good, Mama, but Mr. Jensen doesn't care."

"I'm sure he does, Sara."

"No! He wants Willie to be an engineer."

"You're a good friend, Sara, but they do give him lessons. I'm sure Mr. Jensen cares."

"Maybe, but I think the lessons are Mrs. Jensen's idea."

"Mr. Jensen went to the concert, Sara," Mama pointed out in his favor.

"But he isn't going to let Willie be a musician! And he has to be one!"

Mama looked at her hands. "What we become, Sara, is our choice. If Willie really wants to, he'll be a cellist. Now go, go! Change, if you want to go to the art supply store."

Papa wasn't back when we left. The only art supply store in town was Artco, owned by Mr. Art Reinstein, who was a small, balding man with lips that were perpetually turned up in a slight smile that left creases around his eyes.

"Sara, Mrs. Goldman. What can I help you with today?"

I loved this store, with its crammed shelves stacked with pads and blocks of papers, with its countertop racks of paint tubes, its little drawers full of sticks of pastels and its flat files brimming with exquisite, individual sheets of paper. Whenever I came with Papa, he looked longingly at the pegboard behind the counter hung with tools and T-squares and glues and scissors until he finally picked one tool, one special purchase for the day. I breathed in the air full of paint and said, "I need paints, Mr. Reinstein."

"Well, you're moving up, Sara. What paints have you used before?"

"Mainly pan watercolors at school."

"Not much pigment in school paints. Well, let's see. Let me recommend you start with gouache. It's easier to handle than oil paints, but you can get great subtlety of color. And you can water it down to watercolor consistency if you want, or dilute it just a little and get opaque solids."

"And it's water soluble? It'll wash out of clothes?" Mama asked, ever practical and always oriented to easy clean-up when it came to art.

"Yep, cleans up pretty easily," he said casually and then added, "and you can work on paper, so it's not nearly as expensive as working in oil on canvas."

Mr. Reinstein took me to a display rack where short tubes of gouache were lined up by color. Cadmium red, cadmium yellow, raw umber, burnt umber, burnt sienna, yellow ochre, ultramarine blue, Prussian blue, alizarin crimson, titanium white. I pulled them from the rack and put them on the counter.

"That's a lot of colors," Mama said skeptically. "Do you need all those?"

"It's what Papa told me all artists start with."

"Start with?" Mama asked.

"She's right, Mrs. Goldman," Mr. Reinstein said, but before he could continue, someone else came into the store and he had to excuse himself for a moment.

"Well then, Sara, you'll have to use some of your birthday money from Nana," Mama told me quietly.

"Okay," I said readily.

We went to the counter and as soon as Mr. Reinstein was free, we paid. "And," he said, "I'll throw in some brushes. A gift from me to you, Sara."

How stupid of me. I'd forgotten the brushes. "Thanks, Mr. Reinstein!"

"Thank you, Mama," I said as we left.

"I'm glad you didn't let last night discourage you, Sara,"

"Nothing can do that! I'm going to be an artist, Mama!"

"Then let's celebrate. Let's stop for ice cream!"

The ice cream parlor was another of my favorite haunts in town. It sat in the middle of an asphalt parking lot, a low white building with black letters on the front and glass windows all the way around three sides. The interior was an airy square room, with lots and lots of little white tables and white metal chairs with hot-pink seats. In the summer it brimmed with people, but at the moment it was more or less empty. Because of the windows, there was only one wall that had a place for anything to hang, and that was where all the flavors were listed.

Apple pie, cookie crunch, lemon, peach and strawberry. Mint chocolate chip, Swiss chocolate, coffee chip and plain chocolate chip. Chocolate marshmallow, mocha, chocolate, and bubble gum. I settled for a hot fudge sundae over one scoop of chocolate marshmallow ice cream, one of cherry jubilee and one of bubble gum, topped with whipped cream, sprinkles, peanuts and a cherry. Mama delicately licked at a small French chocolate cone, while I licked repeatedly at a spot on my top lip where the thick fudge kept getting stuck.

Your own mustache, a voice breathed into my ear. I looked up expecting to see Butch leering at me, but no one was nearby.

"Yummy, yes?" Mama asked.

"Huh? Oh, yeah! It's great!"

"Finish up. It's time to go home."

I wiped my lips carefully, looked around once more and followed Mama out to the sidewalk.

"Do you think Papa will be home?" I asked.

"I should hope so! It's almost dark," Mama said.

But when we got home, the house was unlit. Mama hurried inside, flicking on this light and that, calling to Papa.

I set my paints down and looked in the kitchen.

"Michel, Michel?" Mama's call echoed in the empty rooms.

I shivered. "I'm getting a sweater, Mama," I called and dashed up to my room.

There was Papa asleep on my bed with Bear lying on his chest. I backed out and ran to tell Mama. We took off our shoes and, together, climbed the steps barefooted. Mama padded quietly into my room and put her hand gently on Papa's shoulder.

"Michel," she whispered into his ear.

He didn't move, but his breath reassuringly blew a few stray hairs around Mama's cheek. A roll of drawings lay on the floor.

"I'll put them downstairs," I mouthed at Mama and pointed down. She nodded at me as I tiptoed out.

I entered Papa's study and stopped. Lovely Lili was once again taped to the door of the forbidden closet, as if guarding whatever lurked behind it. I tried to keep my eyes away from the penciled face hanging on the door, but it was impossible. I squinted before I really looked, hoping the drawing had some magical ability to repair itself, but no such luck. There it sat with the ballpoint-blue inked handlebar mustache still on its upper lip.

I stuck Papa's drawings quickly next to the closet and sat down on the floor. Lovely Lili stared right back at me. I tried to remember her without the mustache, but it blazed out at me, an open wound bleeding purple ink. I moved my eyes to Eugene. A fourth of him was reconstructed in the original tattoos. I felt goose bumps rise on my arms. I grabbed a sheet of paper from the flat files and left, closing the door behind me. When Eugene was complete, would Papa be healed, or would he too end in some way? I glanced behind me at the door. Please, Papa, I thought, get well.

I returned to the kitchen. Mama's kitchen was always perfect. The sink and stainless fixtures always glistened. Not a crumb sprinkled the floor or the counters. The handles on the refrigerator held not one thumbprint, and I knew that if I opened the oven, it would be spotless and drip free.

I laid my paper on Mama's immaculate kitchen table, got an old bottle for water and a plastic lid to squeeze my paints onto. I closed my eyes and saw the cello cases once again, black and solid in the light-dappled hallway. I watered some paint down and sketched the basic placement and shapes and began mixing colors, closing my eyes to see the image, then transferring it to my paper. I worked without thinking about time until my stomach growled and I realized we had never eaten dinner. I stuck together a bologna sandwich and wolfed it down as I climbed the steps to find Mama.

She was squeezed next to Papa on my bed and they were both sound asleep. Her arm was thrown over Papa, her shoes tossed on the floor, lying at angles. Bear had fallen off the bed. I scooped him up, grabbed my pajamas off a chair, closed the door and went back downstairs. I painted until midnight. The house was hushed. The clock in the kitchen kept rhythm to my heartbeat. I yawned, slipped into my pajamas, stretched out on the sofa with Bear, and instantly fell asleep.

I was dreaming about my painting when I thought I heard something move in the dark room. My eyes popped open. Waking in the middle of the night always fascinated me because it was the only time I saw in black and gray and white like a television show. It was the way Papa must have seen his world for two years.

A sound focused my attention again.

"Who's there?" I called softly. "Mama? Papa?"

No answer came back. I clutched Bear tightly against my chest, cautiously making my way into the front hall. Had I dreamed the noise?

The study door was cracked, a dollop of yellow lamplight sneaking out of it. "Papa? Are you in there?"

Papa's voice answered, "Do not be afraid, little girl."

A chill went through me. "Papa? It's me, Sara!"

"No, no, I am not your *Papa*. It's me," he said. The door opened and the light from the study blinded me. When I could see again, I barely swallowed a scream. Papa stood before me with little scraps of paper stuck to his face. Pieces of Eugene.

"I'm looking for my face," he said, "but I can't seem to find it all."

I barely breathed.

"Can you help me?" he asked.

"Papa threw the rest away," I lied impulsively.

"Away?" Papa's voice sounded lost. "Away? He threw me away?" He sank to the ground. "Not remembered then, not even by *Michel*. Not even a picture of me. Nothing! Forgotten." I thought he sobbed.

"No, no!" I said, and hesitantly put my arm around him. His shoulders heaved, but I couldn't tell if he was crying or not. "I'll show you in the morning. I drew a picture of you and Papa keeps it on his wall. You'll never be forgotten."

Papa's body stilled. "Thank you." He rose and opened the front door as if to leave.

"Wait," I cried out. "Wait!" I ran to him. "Let me wipe your face. You're bleeding," I said without knowing quite why.

I took the edge of my sleeve and wiped at the scraps of paper, before pulling each one off as gently as I could, as if I was cleaning out real wounds. They fluttered to the hall floor. His eyes followed them. The light from the study fell full on his face, illuminating his wild eyes when suddenly, something desperate vanished from them.

"Papa?" I asked. "Go back to bed, Papa."

"Bed? Sara? What are you doing up?"

"I heard you come down for something," I said, trying to keep my voice even.

"I dreamed *Eugène* was looking for me," he said, and rubbed at his eyes.

"Yes, Papa."

"I'll have to finish him soon," he said. "Goodnight." He looked at me and pointed. "Would you mind if I slept with Bear tonight?"

I held the stuffed animal out to him and he clutched it in his hands.

"Goodnight, Papa."

I was about to switch off the light in the study when I stopped and walked over to face the portrait of Eugene. In an instant, I had torn it down. I wanted to tear it into shreds, just as Papa had torn that other portrait so long ago, but instead I rolled it up, labeled it, laid it against the wall, and after hesitating only a moment, grabbed the closet doorknob with both hands and twisted. I jumped as it turned in my hands, its hinges squeaking as it unexpectedly swung open. I grabbed up Eugene and nervously stuffed him behind a few of the many rolls of drawings that lined the walls of Papa's forbidden closet. I closed the closet quickly, and scurried from the room as fast as I could, flicking off the light as I left.

How silent the house was, how dark. A street lamp filtering in through the still open front door was all that lit the hall, but it was enough. I swooped down and grabbed up the little butterflies of paper from the floor where they had fallen, crinkling them in my fists. I stepped to the open door and sent them flying from my hand on the night wind, then closed the door with a firm click.

Squishing Eggs

"Sara?" Mama called in the morning.

I jerked awake on the sofa and rubbed my eyes.

"Sara," she called again.

I wandered to the kitchen, pushed the swinging door open and stuck my head around it. Mama was looking at the kitchen table, covered in my paints and brushes.

"Oh, Mama, I'm so sorry! I meant to clean up, but I fell asleep." I rushed in and began to gather up everything.

"Sara, stop! Stop!"

I hung my head. "I'm sorry, Mama."

"Sara, this is beautiful," Mama said, looking at my painting.

"Really? You aren't mad?"

"Look at me. This," she said, pointing to my painting, "is beautiful. Wait until Papa sees it!"

I got a sick feeling in the pit of my stomach. "Is Papa still upstairs?"

"No, he's already gone into the study. How late were you up doing this?"

"Mama, I'll be right back." I dashed upstairs to the bathroom and locked the door. What was Papa going to do when he saw that Eugene was gone? What was I going to tell him?

Mama knocked on the door. "Are you okay?"

"Yeah, I'll be out in a minute."

I cleaned my face and brushed my teeth and put on fresh pants and a clean shirt.

I didn't want to see Papa, so I darted out the back door, yelling, "I gotta go see Willie."

"Sara, what about breakfast?" Mama called after me. I pumped my legs without looking back. I got to Willie's front door and stood there dumbly, my hand half-raised to knock, when Harriet opened the door.

"Oh," she said. "You didn't knock, did you? Nope, not you! You're too weird to do anything normal."

I wondered why she had opened the door at all, but refused to ask her. I just said, "Is Willie home?"

"Yeah, he's in the shower."

"Will you tell him I'm waiting for him in the tree house?"

"Waiting for what?" she asked, fixing me with a stare. I knew she was trying to provoke me.

"To talk to him. What'd you think, Harriet?"

"Okay, okay, I'll tell him." She closed the door in my face.

I walked slowly around back and climbed the ladder. The safe box stared at me from the rafters. I took out my list. I didn't hesitate, I just started ripping it. I tore at it and tore at it until my hands were shaking. I leaned out the tree house door and tossed handfuls of paper into the air over and over, watching the wind catch them and send them flying in swirls like maple seeds in the spring, until they finally floated to the ground below.

"Hey," Willie called, "whatcha doing, Sara? Why're you tossing that paper all over my yard?"

"It was my list, but I don't want it anymore!" I was breathing hard as I said it.

"Huh? Why not?" he asked, hurrying up the ladder.

"I just don't!"

"What happened?"

I tried to think what to say, but I drew a blank. At last I mumbled, "I'm scared, Willie."

He didn't say anything. We were only twelve. What did he know? What did I?

"I hid the picture of Eugene and I'm afraid to go home," I blurted out.

"Why'd you do that?"

I opened my mouth, and said in a rush of words, "Eugene is haunting Papa and I'm afraid when all the tattoos are back on the drawing, Papa will vanish."

"Aw, Sara, he'd never leave you and your mother. My mom says she's never seen anyone so obviously in love as your mom and dad!"

I shook my head. Willie didn't understand. He didn't live with Papa's memories and stories. He thought they were wonderful, but I knew the black side. "I'm scared, Willie."

"It'll be okay," he said and patted my shoulder.

His touch seemed to bring me out of it a little and I noticed he was all dressed up.

"You going somewhere, Willie?"

"I gotta go to a wedding. My dad's cousin is getting married on a farm some place. The only neat thing about it is they're giving away baby chicks, but you know what my mom says?" He hesitated, then did a perfect imitation of his mother's voice: "'Absolutely not! No smelly little chickens in my house!'"

I laughed.

"That's better. You gotta laugh more, Sara."

"Thanks, Willie."

"Yeah, yeah. You can stay here as long as you want, okay?"

"Thanks again. Have fun!" I said as he climbed down.

"Fun?" he asked from the ground. "Wanna go for me?"

Then he was gone, running to the front of the house. I heard the Caddy take off in a rush of its engine. Willie's life was sure simpler than mine. I looked out one of the tree house windows. Mr. Bellum, two houses over, was hoeing his garden plot. He always grew too many squash and tomatoes and gave them away to everyone on the block. Jerry Blinker's dad was getting a new washing machine delivered. Jerry's mom had died last year. Poor Jerry, he was Harriet's age and nobody talked to him because he talked to himself. A squirrel who had lost its tail somewhere, hopped across the yard, looking more like a bunny than a squirrel. I'd never thought about how much its tail defined a squirrel.

I was hungry, but I didn't want to go home, so I hunched down against a wall and closed my eyes. A cat snarled and then shrieked. A dog barked, presumably at the cat. The tailless squirrel chittered above me in the tree. Every noise made me jump.

Then I heard someone below me on the ladder.

"Sara?" Papa said when he got to the top. "Can I come in?"

"Yeah," I said, but didn't look up.

"Mama sent you breakfast. Hard-boiled egg, grapes, a piece of bread, and here, a bottle of apple juice." He handed me a brown bag.

"Thanks," I said, but I didn't feel like eating with Papa there.

"This is a pretty nice place," he said. "A good design."

It made me smile a little as he said that. Papa, always the architect.

"And you, you made a wonderful painting."

"Thanks."

"You're trying new things. That's good. Very good, Sara!"

"I don't want to draw from my imagination anymore," I announced and looked up at Papa's face. "No more, okay, Papa?"

He stood and looked out over the neighborhood. "This is a good view up here. Nice to be up high above the ground."

"Yes!" I agreed as I cracked the shell on the egg and peeled it until I held a perfect, shiny-skinned oval.

"Nice view. It makes you feel free, doesn't it?" he asked.

Still not a word about Eugene. I chewed on my cheek nervously, and sure enough Papa must have heard my thoughts because, on the very heels of them he said, "*Eugène* would have loved this!"

I should have spoken, but I didn't know what to say. Gulping, I managed to ask, "Papa, are you angry with me?"

"No, Sara. Why would I be angry? Come home when you are ready."

I watched him vanish below the tree house, then reappear and go in the back door.

Had he noticed that Eugene was gone or might he think that Eugene had really just walked away last night? Did he remember last night? Suddenly I was mad! If Butch hadn't drawn on Lovely Lili, none of this would have happened. None of it! We might have been able to go on carefully balancing our lives. But not now! Something had changed. I squeezed my hand into a fist, forgetting that I held the egg until it squished out between my fingers.

Yuck. I wiped some of it off, but the napkin Mama had sent wasn't enough. I climbed down to wash my hands and luckily, nobody was in the kitchen, so I didn't have to explain a handful of mashed egg to anyone.

I was about to retreat back to the tree house when I heard my grandmother's gravelly voice in the front hall.

"Where's Sara?"

"Up in a tree house," Mama said.

"No, I'm not," I called from the kitchen.

Nana came through the door dressed in baggy pants and a big sweat shirt. Gardening days were the only times Nana wasn't dressed like she was going to a lady's luncheon. "It's your day to come help me turn the sod in my garden," she announced. "Go get ready."

I dashed past Mama to change into work clothes. I had forgotten about my promise to help Nana today, but it was just the escape I needed.

Nana lived at the top of a steep hill in a rambling house, more art museum than home. She had traveled widely, and everywhere she went, she collected something beautiful: ivory Mogul figures, Balinese puppets, Japanese vases, Venetian glass,

African Makonde carvings. She was the only person I knew who had been to any of those countries.

We popped into her black Lincoln Continental sedan with the big fins on the back and drove off. Nana was a haphazard driver, beeping at people who got in her way, stopping abruptly if a squirrel crossed the road ahead of her or to watch a dog run in its yard. Papa said she was a hazard, and he was probably right, but I loved it when she sped up to go over a big bump so we could bounce up and down.

"Your mother showed me your painting, Sara! I'd like to frame it for you."

"Really?"

"Really! And I'd like to frame the drawing of your mother, as well."

"She showed that to you?" I asked.

"Actually, your father did. I hate to admit it, but I think you got his talent."

Nana and Papa were always keeping each other at arm's length, so this was about as close to a compliment as Papa was ever going to get from her. She claimed almost everything good about me came from Mama and their family. I supposed there was simply nobody on their side of the family tree who was artistic, so Papa finally got some credit.

"You know," Nana said, "your mother told me about your family history project. Shall I tell you some stories about our relatives while we work in the garden?"

"Sure, that'd be great!" I paused and thought a minute. "Nana, do you know anything about Papa's family?"

I saw her eyes slide to the side to look at me and then flick back to the road.

"Not much, darling."

"He won't talk about them."

Nana pursed her lips. "Well, you know, most people who survived the war don't talk about it. It's hard for them."

"No, Nana, he talks about the war, about hiding, about the people who hid with him all the time. He just won't talk about his family!"

She pulled into her driveway and stopped the car without commenting. I could see she was thinking about what she should say to me.

"Nana," I asked quickly, "do you think I should let him tell me his stories or not?"

She looked at me. "What does your mother say?"

"I want to know what you think," I said evasively.

"I don't know, Sara. Do you think there is any harm in it?"

I bit my lip. If I told her the truth, she might like Papa even less, but I needed advice.

"I've been thinking about that. When he tells me the stories, sometimes I think he gets his memories mixed up with real time and that's bad."

"Yes, it is," she said and waited for me to go on.

"But if he can't tell me, then the stories are still there, building up in his head, and that's gotta be bad, too."

"Yes, that could be bad, too."

"So what do I do, Nana?"

She wrapped her arms around me. "I don't know, Sara. I guess you should do what your heart tells you is right, because I don't think our heads can figure it out."

This was a first, Nana being sentimental. I pulled out of her hug and saw pity written on her face.

"Why don't you like Papa?" I asked, surprising both her and me.

"Like your father? I like Michel, but, well, listen, Sara, when you're a mother someday, you'll understand. Every mother wants her child to be happy and to have an easy life."

"And life with Papa is hard," I said knowingly. "Real hard."

"Yes, I'm afraid it is."

We didn't speak as we hacked at the ground with hoes and rakes. The hard work was what I needed. I found peace working the earth: digging up an earthworm, watching a potato bug roll along on its little legs, discovering a baby mantis so young it was barely green. I was pulling weeds in my work-gloved hands when, as if the conversation had never ended, I said, "Nana, you know how you said you wanted Mama to be happy?"

"Yes."

"Well, part of the time she isn't, but when Papa is right, she is. It's like she's singing all the time, when he's right."

Nana stopped hoeing and said, "Is that so? Well, I'm glad. Now if we could only make him right all the time!"

We worked the rest of the day without mentioning Papa again. Nana told me about her great uncle who had taken a barge down the Mississippi all the way to Texas where he bought up land on which to graze cattle. And the land turned out to have oil on it. She told me about one of her brothers, the black sheep of the family, who wanted to marry a lady their mother didn't like. He got so mad he ran off with one of their cars and parked it at the edge of the Ohio River, leaving a note on the front seat that he had jumped in. They dragged and dragged the river for him, but his body never showed up. His mother mourned him and his father couldn't speak his name for months. A year later his mother received a letter. It had all been a prank to get back at her. He was alive and well, living on the West Coast.

"I'm gonna write all this down when I get home," I said.

"That'd be good," Nana said. "I'm glad I got to tell it to you."

By the time Nana drove me home, my hands were blistered, my legs were sore, my face was dirty, but it had been a satisfying day. The car rolled along, the edges of the world speeding by my window as I thought about how Nana kept all her stories where they belonged, in the past. Then again, they were just stories, not real memories like Papa's. I mulled on that thought. Mama insisted that Papa's stories weren't real, but when he told them, they were very real to me. I could see the visitors to his hole, could hear their voices, feel their glances, because Papa remembered them, knew them, had maybe even loved some of them. How did Mama know the people Papa spoke of weren't real? They were more real than the cutout people Nana described.

"Well, Sara, here we are," Nana said as the car pulled up in front of my house. "Maybe you can come back next weekend."

"Thanks, Nana." I kissed her cheek and hopped out.

When she pulled off, I sat down on the front stoop to think some more.

The problem was that when Papa talked about his friends and acquaintances from the hole under the barn floor, he wasn't really the Papa I knew. He was distant and changed, although the people he spoke of took on real lives. So which Papa was the real one? I couldn't reconcile it, and soon I got hungry and wanted a snack. A note was taped to the front door: *Papa and I have gone to the store. Back soon.*

I lifted a rock in the flower bed and picked up the extra key. I was standing in the hall, debating what I was going to eat, when the study seemed to call to me. The door was open and I walked slowly to it. I stepped in and my stomach sank. All my drawings were gone! Not one left!

In that single moment, all the contentment of the day shattered and I sank to the floor and cried. Papa had taken his revenge. I stayed there until I ran out of tears, and in a daze stood, and went into the kitchen. I poured a glass of milk and, like an automaton, I drank it in big, regular, perfectly timed gulps. Then I sat stiffly and waited, my mind at a halt.

Time passed, the clock ticked, and as if from a great distance away, I heard the door open. Papa and Mama came in laughing, arms loaded with packages.

"Sara?" Mama said. "Sara, what's the matter?"

"Where are they, Papa?" I demanded. "What'd you do with my drawings? Did you rip them up? Did you throw them out?"

He came to me and knelt down so his face was level with mine. "Sara, I put them away. You said you didn't want to draw from your imagination any more. I rolled them up and put them where they belong, that's all. In the closet."

I felt cold. Dispassionately I asked, "You put them in the closet? Can I have them back?"

"Of course. Whenever you want them."

"Papa, do you want to know where Eugene is?"

Momentarily his eyes glazed over and then he said, "No, leave him be." He stood and started putting groceries away.

I breathed again. I could feel the color coming back into my numbed face. I could feel life imbue my fingers with movement. Papa didn't want Eugene back!

"Did you know Nana is going to frame my painting?" I asked.

Papa glanced at Mama and said, "That's very nice."

"She said I'm talented like you, Papa. Isn't that nice, too?"

He gave me a funny look and a half-smile. I really wanted Papa and Nana to like each other, and I had decided on a mission to make it happen.

"Well, I'd better go do some homework. I have my family tree to do."

"Did Nana give you lots of information?" Mama asked.

"Yep, lots!"

Mama went outside to empty the garbage and Papa said, "So, Nana told you many family stories?"

"Yep."

"That's nice, Sara. Very nice."

I watched his face as he drummed his fingers on the table.

"Papa, will you at least tell me your mother's and father's names? It would help a lot."

He raised his eyes without moving his head. "My father was *Solomon* and my mother was *Gertrude*."

"Thanks, Papa," I said and kissed his cheek.

"And my sisters, they were *Sara* and *Berta*."

"So you named me after your sister?"

"Yes."

"And your grandmother," I said, pushing for whatever else I could get.

"Lilian." He stood up. "That is all, Sara. The rest is lost to the grave."

As soon as he went outside to help Mama with more bags of groceries, I headed for my room and my dictionary of names. Lilian sounded a lot like Lili to me. I flipped the pages and checked. Yes, they might be variants of the same name. Lilian meant *lily* in Greek and Latin, but Lila was a variant, too, and it meant *she is mine* in Hebrew. And Lilly was also a variant of Elizabeth, which meant *God's oath* in Hebrew coming from Elisheba. It was confusing. But, if Papa's grandmother had been Lili, maybe it was she, not a little wisp of a girl hiding from death in a hole, who had given Bear to Papa.

I put my name dictionary away. Papa had found the book for me when I was five and I had just begun to read. What had he said when he handed it to me? What had it been? *To find everyone in*, that was what he had said to me. Yes, that was it.

I wished I hadn't torn up my copy of the list, because all of a sudden, I wondered if all the names of Papa's story people had meanings I could have found in my name book? How many could I remember? I got out a pad and started a new list of whomever I could recall. *Marcella. Perach*, I remembered because of the story that went with it.

Perach was the girl who smelled of peach blossoms and arrived in a wet spring when water came seeping into the hole. *Seff*, yes, that was another. Papa told of how his eyes glowed like a wolf's in the dark. I had almost forgottten *Seabern*, one of the strangest names Papa had mentioned; *Seabern* who had climbed from the hole in broad daylight. Papa had known that the soldiers would be waiting, but as he listened from below, he heard not the rapid fire of guns, but shouts and hollers as something growled and snarled. And afterwards, blood had dripped through the floor boards, bright and hoary.

I stopped. Every name I remembered went with a story I had already heard. I sighed. In my fury at Eugene's intrusion into our lives, I had cut and torn everybody to ribbons, and now the ones I didn't know were lost to me. What had I done? I lay down on my stomach and closed my eyes and felt myself drifting off. No, no! I couldn't go to sleep! My family tree was due all too soon. I grabbed my notebook and started my homework. I made the list of whomever I knew from each of my families. Mama's side was long. Papa's was short. On Mama's side I wrote the dates of her relatives' births and deaths. On Papa's side, I figured out the dates for Sara and Berta, but for Lilian,

Solomon and Gertrude, I could put nothing. I closed my pad and sat up. The assignment sheet said I needed a cover and I knew exactly what I wanted to put on it.

Mama and Papa were listening to the radio in the kitchen.

"Can I paint the two of you for the cover of my project?" I asked.

"What do you think, Lea?" Papa asked. "Shall we be a famous topic of our future, famous-artist daughter?"

Mama laughed. "Of course. After dinner, okay, Sara?"

I said that was fine, but while Papa listened to the radio and Mama chopped up celery and onions, I drew. The sound of the radio filled in the background of my world, but whenever I stopped, the faces of my father's stories filled up my eyes. Then I would return to my drawing, and my parents would fill my world again.

A Cold Black Gun

Bright and early Sunday morning, Mr. Jensen hammered on our front door instead of using the doorbell. It was seven-thirty and I had just groggily wandered downstairs, thinking about an early start to homework still unfinished. I peeked through the spy window on the door and saw Mr. Jensen, sparkling clean in his good Sunday suit.

"Hi," I said as I opened the door. What could Willie's father want at this hour?

"Is your father home? I need to talk to him."

"Uh, he hasn't come downstairs yet. Can I tell him something when he does?" I asked nervously.

"Aw, shoot! I was trying to catch him early. Maggie's got my day so filled up with stuff, I don't know when I'll get another chance."

"Well, he'll probably be here all day. Maybe I could tell him when you'll be back," I suggested.

Mr. Jensen counted off on his fingers: church, lunch with his mother-in-law, a visit with Maggie's uncle which might take hours, because the old buzzard could talk forever. Yep, a short break around four-thirty before they went to the church fundraiser. "How about quarter till six? Tell him to call it an appointment, okay?"

"I'll try, Mr. Jensen," I started to say, but he was already rumbling off, muttering under his breath.

Mr. Jensen sure didn't seem very happy with his Sunday, but Willie was probably taking advantage of all those family visits to fill in the gaps in his family tree project.

I worked on algebra for about an hour before Papa and Mama ambled downstairs. Papa looked sleep tossed, but Mama had already combed her hair and was in her deep-blue fluffy robe.

She went straight for the coffee pot and started it percolating, and Papa went to the door for the paper, which was always at the end of the sidewalk.

I had a bad feeling as I watched him. When he was the Architect, he never set foot on the sidewalk with a hair out of place, but this morning his hair was hanging askew and his face wasn't yet shaven.

"Papa, I'll get the paper," I said.

"Why, thank you, Sara." He smiled.

That was good. "Oh yeah, Willie's father wants to make an appointment at quarter to six to talk to you."

"On a Sunday?"

I shrugged. I danced down the walk in my bare feet and grabbed up the paper. It was slightly damp from an early drizzle, but the sun was coming out now. One bird, then another chirped somewhere in the light fog that was rising as the day warmed up. With any luck the mist would burn away and leave a brilliant spring day.

"Here you go," I said.

"Thanks. This looks like it's going to be a great day."

"Yes. Papa, what art museums have you been to?"

"Hmm, why?"

"Well, I want to make a list of where I should visit some-day. Nana says to be sure to go to the Taj Mahal. And the Parthenon. And the Louvre. And the Prado."

"Don't leave out the Sistine Chapel in the Vatican, or the British Museum, or Pompeii."

"Have you been to them?" I asked.

"Or the Museo de Antropologia in Mexico City!"

"Which ones have you been to?" I asked him.

"The Metropolitan in New York. The National Gallery in Washington. There are so many. When I get older, I will see all the great museums, Sara."

"Can I come?" I asked excitedly.

"I wish, I wish upon starlight, that we both get to go! Wait, what's that sound? Here quick, upstairs, under the beds!" he said, switching place and time so abruptly, I couldn't even back away before he grabbed my arm and dragged me towards the stairs. I struggled against him, grasping at the door frames, try-ing to grab the banister, twisting away, but he was too strong.

"It's too late to run, Sara. Too late! Just come, quickly!"

"Papa, it's me! It's me," I screeched, hitting at him ineffectu-ally. "Let go, let go!"

Mama must have heard us because she came scrambling up the steps.

"Michel, let her go! Let her go," she cried out.

"Too late to run," he said again.

Mama grabbed his arm and dug her fingers into it, but he swatted her away. "I won't let you hurt my sister!" he screamed. "She has to hide!"

Mama stopped to take a deep heave of air before she said as calmly as she could, "Michel, Sara and I need to eat now. Please, it's time for breakfast. She must eat before they come, mustn't she?"

"Eat?"

"Yes, it will be the last time she has a chance for a good meal," Mama said slyly.

"Oh, yes, perhaps. But then it will be time to hide!"

"Yes, of course," Mama said. She clutched my hand and we walked down the stairs with our breath sucked in.

I looked back and Papa was sitting on the top step, staring into someplace in his past.

Mama hurried us into the kitchen and sat down heavily in a chair, her head thrown back, her eyes closed tightly. After a few minutes, she got up and dialed a number. "Hello, yes, Dr. Pine please. What? He's away for the weekend? Then who is taking his calls?" A pause. "Yes? All right. Thank you."

"Do you think we can get Papa to go to the hospital with us?"

"I don't think so, Mama."

"No, nor do I." She picked up the phone and dialed again. "Mother, could you come get ..."

"No!" I said and pressed the buttons on the phone to cut off the conversation. "I'm not leaving."

"Sara, I don't think it's safe for you to be here."

"I'm staying. Papa won't hurt us! He's lost somewhere, and we have to bring him home. That's all," I said stubbornly.

I went back into the hall and heard the bathroom shower running. Over the noise of the running water, Papa sang loudly in his off-key, slightly nasal voice. After a few minutes I heard him run the water in the sink and I knew he was shaving.

"See, Mama, he's back."

"For how long, Sara? For how long?"

When he came downstairs he was in neatly pressed casual pants and a plaid shirt. His hair was combed back. His eyes were sparkling bright.

"So what's for this breakfast I heard you were cooking? A special meal for this day, is it?"

"Sara, see if Willie is home," Mama said, nodding towards the Jensen house.

"They went to church," I said.

"Perhaps Willie stayed home to do homework. He does that sometimes, doesn't he?" She wanted me out of Papa's reach.

"No!" Nana's words came back to me. Decide with your heart. "Papa, I still need some information for my project."

"What?"

"For my family tree."

"Sara!" Mama hissed.

"I need to know how old your mama and papa were when they were killed," I said boldly.

He brought his head up. "They were thirty-three, Sara."

"Yes? What happened?" I asked. Mama's face was furious, but it was too late to turn back. "I need to know."

"The soldiers came. *Papa* always said they would come." Papa's eyes drifted away, then jerked back. "Must you know this?"

"Yes, Papa, I must." I crossed my fingers, hoping I had made the right decision.

His mouth opened and closed several times before he began in a dull voice. "It was late at night. They always came with the darkness. Always. *Thrump, thrump.* There were ten of them, big, bright-haired men who brought the night, the final night. *Papa* had his gun out. It was dark, heavy, black. *Maman* hurried us upstairs. We heard *Papa* open the door. *Thrump.* We heard voices shouting. *Maman* pushed me under my bed and I rolled back until I hit the wall. She pushed a big trunk in after me. I knew that if anything happened I was to make it to the edge of the town to a certain farmer. It was all arranged. All inevitable. I could hear *Maman* trying to hide *Sara* and *Berta,* but too late, too late!

"*Thrump*," Papa's voice said again. "*Thrumpp*, and then the shots. *Un. Deux. Trois. Quatre. Thrumppp.*"

The clock ticked in the kitchen. Tears rolled down Papa's face. "It happened like that for the *Salomons*, the *Tibbons*, the *Lilienthals*. It happened. *Thrump.* And my family, everyone was covered by the darkness. *Thrump.* Two little bodies on the floor. *Maman,* eyes wide. *Papa,* brains oozing on the floor. *Thrumppp.* I was alone. Alone!"

Silence cradled the room and those gory images from my Papa's past engraved themselves on my eyes, on my mind until I felt like I would vomit.

"But you got to the farmer, Michel," Mama said, her teeth clamped together so that she spoke through them.

He looked at her. "I stared at the gun, touched it, still sticky with my family's blood. Then I tucked it under my shirt where it weighed against my lungs as if it would press the breath from me, too. I don't remember how I got to the farmer in the dark. I have no memory at all of anything except the image of my father and the heft of the heavy, black gun against my ribs."

I went up to Papa and hugged him, swallowing the bile that threatened my throat. "And do you know, Sara," he asked, "do you know? They shot them with my *Papa's* own gun! With the big, dark gun with which he thought he could protect us. Will you put that in your report?"

His voice was icy, but I felt his hot tears fall on my face.

"No, Papa, no! I won't tell anyone."

He shook me off, picked his jacket off the coat rack in the hall and went out the door.

Mama sat down with her hands in her lap and stared at me. When she spoke, it was in a voice so harsh I could barely understand her. "Why did you do that, Sara? Why?"

I couldn't explain. She wouldn't understand. If Papa didn't speak about it, his brain might explode, he might end. As if in a dream, I wandered absently into the study. The closet door stood wide open. Roll after roll of drawings leaned in neat rows lining the walls, filling the closet. *Eugène, Eugène,* the small voice called and with a start, I discovered myself pawing at the drawings, knocking them aside, searching for Eugene, but he wasn't there.

Mama grabbed my hands. "Sara, what are you doing? You're making a mess of Papa's closet! Stop! You aren't supposed to be in there! You know that."

"I'm looking for something important and it isn't here!"

"Put it all back," Mama said. Her voice was calm, but I could tell she was mad at me.

I sank down on the closet floor. I was tired and afraid and I wanted Papa to come back. Maybe I had done the wrong thing. What if he never came back? I sat there a long time before I slowly began to re-stack the rolls of drawings. As I moved each one, I looked for the word *Eugene* that I had scribbled on the outside of the roll, but it wasn't there.

When I finished I went to find Mama. I looked in the kitchen, I looked in the living room, I looked in her bedroom. She was nowhere. Then I heard a small whimper from the bathroom.

"Mama, are you in there?"

"Go away," her broken voice said. "Go away!"

"Please, Mama. Please, it's gonna be okay. Please come out," I begged. I felt tears in my own eyes.

"Go away, Sara."

I slumped to the floor and cried with my forehead pressed against the bathroom door. I rubbed at my eyes and wiped my nose on my sleeve, but I couldn't stop crying. Finally the door nudged at me from within.

"Sara, stop crying," Mama said.

I slid back a little and Mama squeezed out into the hall. Sniffling herself, she sat on the floor next to me and took my hand.

"You're all soggy, Sara."

"Yeah. So are you."

We sat there without speaking for a long time.

At last, as if from far away, Mama spoke. "It was autumn when Papa got off a bus in our town, carrying a brown paper bag with everything he owned in it. He walked over to Old Mr. Jensen's filling station and asked for a job. Old Mr. Jensen was a jolly, fat man with a little black goatee. He looked at your Papa and said, 'Well now, son, can you pump gas?' Papa asked him how hard it could be, and Old Mr. Jensen laughed and told him not too hard. After he gave Papa the job, Papa registered at my high school. That was the fall I tried to pass my driver's test for the third time so I could get my license. Nana had sent me off in her car to take the test and the sheriff made me pull up and put gas in the tank. So there came your Papa, with his wild, long hair and skeletal face. The sheriff sat up and said, 'Who's that?' I told him it was just some new boy at the school who was living in the rooming house in town. 'War boy, huh?' the sheriff grumbled.

"That was the first time I knew that Papa had survived the war. It was the first time I really thought about him at all." Mama stopped with a distant look on her face.

"Mama, what did he have in his brown bag?"

"Oh, some clothes from a war relief agency, Bear and a gun."

"A gun? Was it the same gun?" I asked, my heart pounding.

"I don't know, Sara. Today was the first time Papa ever talked about how his family was murdered. Perhaps it was the same."

"Does he still have it, Mama?"

"It's on a shelf in our closet, still wrapped in a brown paper bag," she said.

I ran into their room with Mama on my heels. "Is it there? Look, Mama, please!"

She reached up and pulled down a lumpy bag. "Yes, still here, Sara."

We sat on her bed with that bag between us, a blotch on the neatly made coverlet.

I toyed with the edge of the brown paper, my fingers turning it back slowly. Inside, buried under bits and pieces of Eugene, was an ugly black barrel.

"Death in a bag," I mumbled.

Mama grabbed it from me, closed the lip of the bag and hurriedly stuck it back on the shelf. "Don't say things like that, Sara. And don't ever touch it again! I would never have let him keep it all this time if I'd known what it was."

"Let's throw the whole thing away, right now!" I said.

She looked down at me, and touched my cheek. "Sara, no matter what happens, we can't do that. Papa has to do it himself, or it won't mean anything, will it? Isn't that why you asked him about his family? So that he would face what happened?"

I looked up at her. My eyes felt swollen from crying and I imagined they were bloodshot. Hers were.

"Mama, what if I was wrong? What then?"

"I don't know, Sara. Let's wash our faces and go outside to plant some flower seeds."

"Mama, how can we?"

"If we can't go on, Sara, how will Papa be able to?"

There was no answer to that. Mama had a lot of seeds and we worked hard putting them into the ground. Neither of us was hungry. We tugged at places where grass and dandelions invaded our beds and examined the heads of leaves pushing through the earth. The tips of daffodils were up an inch already. Early crocus were budding. Mama cleaned the birdfeeder and we filled it with seed.

Preparing to replace old life with new? Lovely Lili's voice asked accusingly. *You can't forget us. Your Papa won't let you.*

Go away, I thought back, but I knew she wouldn't.

When Mama looked at her watch, it was four-thirty. We stood and stretched and went in to wash up. I had just begun to read a little history when the doorbell rang. Mr. Jensen was there.

"So, did you tell your father?" he asked.

"Uh, yes," I said.

"Well, could you get him?" Mr. Jensen asked impatiently.

I was standing there debating what to tell him, when Papa walked up the sidewalk.

"Hello, Wally," he said to Mr. Jensen, "what can I do for you?"

"Well, I got to talk some business with you."

"Fine, fine, come into my study. Sara, ask Mama to get us some coffee."

I was left staring curiously at the closed study door. Papa was acting like nothing had happened. He had even remembered his appointment.

"Mama," I cried out excitedly, "Papa's back! He's in the study with Mr. Jensen and they want coffee."

She came out of the kitchen drying her hands and looked towards the closed door.

"And a little coffee cake, too," she said, as if it was some sort of celebration.

Maybe it was. I crossed my fingers.

Mama knocked with the tray of goodies and Papa came to the door, kissed her cheek and took it from her with a thank you and a nod.

I tried to go on reading, but couldn't sit still. I flicked on the radio, but the reception was lousy. I got up and walked up the stairs and back down. I brushed at my hair. I even straightened my notebook. Finally Papa and Mr. Jensen came out and shook hands and Mr. Jensen left.

Papa said, "Well, what are you up to, Sara?"

"Uh, what did Mr. Jensen want?"

"Well, his wife wants to put a music room on the back of their house, and he wants me to design it, if he has to do it."

"For Willie?"

"I suppose. He thinks it's a waste of time, but she is really adamant about it. So Mr. Jensen decided, if Willie was to get a music room, he should get himself a really fancy game room. Then Harriet wanted her own bathroom and Mr. Jensen added a bar into the mix. Suddenly, he had a huge project."

"Are you gonna do it, Papa?" I asked.

"Well, that depends."

"On what?"

"On who wins the argument, Mr. Jensen or Mrs. Jensen."

"Huh? What's that mean, Papa?"

"It means, *Mademoiselle Sara*, that Mr. Jensen is using the extras as a way of bluffing Mrs. Jensen out of the music room."

"Oh," I said.

"Yes, well, we'll see. Now what does Mama have planned for dinner?"

"Papa, are you upset with me?"

"For what, Sara?" he asked.

"About, you know, what I asked you before? I mean you walked away and well, I was afraid."

"Of what? I went to survey a site and talk to Mr. Sirks about the new library. I think they're going to build it near Piker's Stream. I want them to do it in stone, right up against the rock face there. I want lots of windows framed in cherry wood. The floors will all be smooth limestone that will be cool in summer and hold heat in the winter. I'm thinking of a buff tile roof. Can you see it, Sara?"

I closed my eyes. "That would be pretty, Papa" I said, holding the image behind my eyelids.

"Yes, and peaceful. A library should be quiet and peaceful, don't you think?"

"Yeah, peaceful is nice."

"Yes, nice. That was what I used to think when it was quiet at night. Peaceful. No noise, no trucks, no pigs snorting above me. I used to imagine that everyone was sleeping safely in their beds, when it was peaceful."

I didn't want to go where Papa was taking me. "Come on, come see what Mama and I did. We planted the gardens," I said and led him outside. "We're gonna get peonies this year, you know, like Nana has in her garden? The big, pink ones with the touch of red along the edges of their petals."

"I love the smell of flowers."

"Papa, would you mind if I planted some lilies for Lovely Lili? Like a marker for her."

"But Sara, you only put out markers for the dead," he said, "and she's not dead."

"She isn't?" I asked.

"No, she isn't! She is just hiding in the closet." He winked at me, laughed and stepped inside.

Don't Breathe, Don't Twitch

As I entered the school halls before first period Monday morning, the usual prattle of girls about their boyfriends, and boys about sports and their triumphs with girls, didn't even irritate me. Anxiety, nervousness and relief at being out of my house left me in a daze. Amy trotted up and we walked to art class together. I gritted my teeth as I entered. Butch sat in the corner with his feet up on the table grinning dumbly at Marcia. His eyes met mine for a minute and he went back to his quarry. In that moment I hated Butch. In that moment, I swore again I'd get even with him.

Mr. Paleri was late. A neatly dressed woman followed him in. "Ladies and gentlemen!" he said. "Uh hum!"

Everybody chattered on.

He tried again. "May I have your attention, please!"

The noise level dropped, but the class was a long way from giving Mr. Paleri their silent attention. He waited a minute more before he dimmed the lights. Everyone got quiet at last. I had my eyes fixed on Butch. I wished I could call one of Papa's characters down on him. The Bringer of the Evil Eye! I closed my eyes to make the wish, but Mr. Paleri broke my concentration.

"All right, class. This is Mrs. Morris. She is from an arts school in New York City, and she is here to tell you about a very special opportunity for the summer. Please give her your attention."

Mrs. Morris stepped forward. She wore horn-rimmed glasses and a suit, but despite her neat appearance, I noticed the tell-tale mark of the artist on her. She had paint beneath her finger-nails and more paint had stained her fingertips.

"Hello, everyone. I am the chair of the selection committee and I am meeting with different junior high and high school art departments and asking them to nominate one student for a full scholarship to study visual art at our school during the summer. It includes tuition, a supervised stay in a dormitory and all your meals. You will get to take special classes and tours of museums and art galleries and in the past, everyone has gone home with a fabulous portfolio of pieces."

Amy nudged me and leaned over to whisper, "That is so cool!"

"Yeah!" I agreed.

Mr. Paleri said, "I have already made my recommendation. I'll be speaking with the lucky person about submitting a selection of pieces for review while the rest of you work on your projects."

I could hear everyone stop breathing. *Hold your breath. Don't make a sound. Don't breathe, even if you turn blue,* the voice spoke to me. My heart was pounding.

Everyone got up and went to get their supplies. Mr. Paleri continued talking to Mrs. Morris. I passed close enough to hear him say, "Do you mind waiting a few minutes before I introduce you to the student? I have to take care of something first."

I went back to my seat with my paper and pencils, but I couldn't start. I nudged Amy back. "It'd better not be Butch!"

139

"You're kidding, right?" Amy asked. "Butch isn't an artist."

I looked up. Mr. Paleri and Mrs. Morris were still talking. Mr. Paleri always used his hands when he talked, and he was gesturing at the artwork that was still on the walls from the show. I looked at the big, blank hole where Lovely Lili had hung. It wasn't going to be me, that was for sure.

"I hope you get it, Amy," I said, looking at her pot that sat on the table in front of us. "You do really nice work."

I looked back down at my paper.

"Sara," Mr. Paleri called to me, "can I speak with you a moment about Friday night?"

My stomach dropped. What else could go wrong? A reprimand in front of everyone, including Mrs. Morris.

"Yeah, I guess so."

We walked into his office which was cluttered with paper and supplies, stacked in awkward piles because there had been a small flood in our supply closet.

Mrs. Morris was walking around the classroom talking to everyone else. He cleared his throat.

"Mr. Paleri, I really don't want to talk about this! I'm sorry."

"No, I'm sorry, Sara. You should have won first prize and I feel terrible that your drawing was defaced."

"Thanks," I said.

"You understand, I tried to explain to the judges that you were an exceptional artist?"

"It's okay, Mr. Paleri. My Papa says I won anyway, because the judges thought it was so good, they didn't believe I had done it."

"Well, now, your father is a very smart man."

"Yes, he is," I said, looking directly at Mr. Paleri for the first time that morning. "Can I go now?"

"No, Sara, you can't. Wait here one minute." He left and walked towards Mrs. Morris. Amy waved to me through the glass that surrounded the office. I waved back and shrugged. I just wanted to go back to work.

Mr. Paleri and Mrs. Morris came into the office. "Sara, this is Mrs. Stephanie Morris and I particularly wanted her to meet you."

"Hi," I said.

"I didn't see your work on the walls," she said.

She opened her mouth to say something else, but I burst out before she could. "I took my drawing home. Anyway, the judges didn't like it."

She looked at me with her head thrust to one side. "Yes, Mr. Paleri explained that to me, but he also told me you are a wonderful artist! Would you like to apply for a place in our program?"

"Me?"

She smiled and nodded.

"Uh, what do I have to do?" I asked. I twisted around for a second and saw Amy. She grinned at me and gave me a thumbs up sign.

"Well, you would have to send slides of about ten pieces of your choice. And then there's an application form with an essay and a recommendation from Mr. Paleri and one other teacher." I didn't notice she had stopped speaking at first because the voice was saying, *Don't Breathe. Don't Breathe. It might all evaporate!*

"What? Oh, yeah! I'd love to try." I knew a smile was plastered across my face. "Thank you, Mrs. Morris! Thank you, Mr. Paleri!"

"One more thing, Sara," Mr. Paleri said. "Usually Mrs. Morris gets to see the nominee's work. Do you think we could drop by after school and see your art?"

"Uh, gee, well, I guess so. Can I call Mama just to be sure?"

"Of course, here, you use my phone right now and we'll go out and talk to some of the other kids." Mr. Paleri pointed to his desk where the phone sat under a pile of papers.

I dialed my number and watched the rotary spin as I put my finger in each hole and twisted. The phone rang and rang, but Mama was out.

Mr. Paleri came in. "Is it okay?"

"Yeah, sure," I said. "What time?"

"About four?"

"Yeah, that's okay," I said. That would give me time to run home and find where Papa had put my work. I could try calling at lunch and maybe Papa would be home and would have it all out before I got there. Maybe.

In the Family

Lunch came and went without anybody answering at home. Papa was usually in his study at lunchtime, but not today. I chewed the eraser off the end of my pencil in math and then came history.

And of course, with the kind of luck I was having, my name was the first one out of Mrs. Bancroft's mouth.

"Sara, we haven't heard from you yet about your family history."

Willie gave me a quick look and watched me go to the head of the class. Butch snickered like he always did whenever he saw me. His father was a town councilman and his mother headed the garden club. His grandfather had built a big business in haberdashery and all the men in town bought their clothes there, still. Butch had an utterly complete family tree back to the Pilgrims. He had photographs and even diaries and letters, all meticulously preserved.

"Well," I mumbled.

"Speak up, Sara. We can't hear you if you mumble."

I raised my head and looked at Willie. "Well, I'm still doing research. I pretty well have my mother's family finished, but my father's is a little harder. A lot of them died in the war."

Mrs. Bancroft cleared her throat. "Yes, your mother mentioned that, but you must know something about them. What can you tell us?"

I closed my eyes and Lovely Lili's voice said, *Go ahead. We're all family, aren't we?*

My mouth opened; my voice spoke. I looked at Willie. His eyes were wide and he was shaking his head at me really hard.

"Well, well, that's very interesting," Mrs. Bancroft said, and I had no idea what she was talking about. "You may sit down now, Sara."

When the bell rang, I rushed out of the room. I practically ran down the hall towards my locker, but Willie caught up to me, grabbed my arm and forced me to stop. "Sara, how could you?"

"Huh? What?"

"You said that Lovely Lili and Rudi and some other guys I'd never heard of were your father's family? That's not true, is it?"

"Huh? I did?"

"Don't you even know what you said?" he asked.

My stomach flip-flopped and I didn't dare open my mouth to say, no I didn't remember. I shook my head at Willie, my mouth clamped shut, and ran into the girl's bathroom.

Willie yelled in, "Come on, Sara, come outta there."

"Go away," I screamed.

I locked myself in a stall and banged my head against the wall. It was all Mrs. Bancroft's fault. She shouldn't have pushed me so hard! What had come over me? Was I going crazy like Papa?

Amy came in and called softly, "Sara, Willie's worried about you. He said you were crying in here."

I rubbed at my eyes and stepped out. "No, I'm not! What time is it, Amy?"

She looked at the delicate little gold watch she always wore and said, "Almost three-thirty"

"What! Oh, no! I gotta go. I was supposed to be home already."

I ran past her down the hall, past Willie, slammed out the front doors, and raced down the sidewalk, bumping anybody in my way, mumbling apologies as I plowed through them. My back pack was heavy with the books I hadn't put in my locker and I was panting after three blocks. I had to slow down, and Willie caught up to me.

"Sara, why'd you run away?"

Now tears were pouring down my face. "I told a lie! I told Mr. Paleri my parents said it was okay for him and this lady to drop by and see my artwork. And it was a lie! I never got Mama or Papa. I don't even know if they're home and I don't have my work ready."

My words were coming out all mushy and chopped up, but Willie took my back pack and said, "I'll carry it. Run. You're fast. Take off your shoes and run."

I dropped my shoes on the ground at his feet and took off. I hoped Mr. Paleri would be late, really late. He was usually late!

The front door was open and as I stepped through I knew it was too quiet. I closed the door and called out, "Mama, Papa?"

Papa came out of the study, his clothes all awry. My heart sank all the way to the bottom of my feet.

"Papa, I need your help."

"Yes, for what?" he asked softly.

"Papa, where are my drawings? Please, please, help me find them!"

"Oh, I sent them off with Achichud the Riddler. He's hiding them from the soldiers for me. No one must know who has hidden here in the hole with me."

I grabbed his arms and yelled, "No, Papa, not right now! You said they were in the closet. Please, Papa, please, come back! Help me find them!"

"Too late, I sent them already. They could not stay here any longer. It is not safe."

I sank to the floor in tears. Not today, not now! I got up slowly and shoved past Papa. "Go up to bed," I called over my shoulder as I put my hand on the knob to the closet door. It was locked. I twisted it and pulled at it, but it was hopeless.

As if someone had punched a button, Papa reacted. "No!" he screamed. "They are all hiding! Do not open that door!" He yanked at me as I clung to the knob.

"Stop it, Papa! I have to get my drawings outta there. Where's the key?"

"No, no, I won't ever give you the key. The soldiers will find them if you open the door!"

I ignored him and yanked harder as he grabbed me around the waist and tried to carry me out of the room. I kicked wildly and hit at him with the flats of my hands, but it was like a fly attacking Godzilla.

"Stop it, stop it, Papa! Lili and Zara and Etan want out! Please, Papa, just let them see the sun for a few minutes."

Papa put me down just as the doorbell rang. He backed away, swinging his head from side to side, his hair flying wildly across his eyes.

I yelled out, "Just a minute."

I sidestepped Papa and closed the door to the study. Sobbing, I dashed to the kitchen to splash water in my face. Where, oh where, was Mama? But even if she came through the back door right that minute, it was too late.

I combed my fingers through my hair and went to the front door. I'd have to tell the truth, and then it would be over. No one would want me in a special program for special kids who wanted to be artists. Nobody would want a liar.

Mrs. Morris and Mr. Paleri were standing there chatting pleasantly. To them the world looked peachy keen on a bright sunny afternoon. To me the day was shrouded in grays, like Papa's study when the curtains were drawn, like his childhood world beneath the barn floor under the pig trough.

"Well, well, here we are," Mr. Paleri said. "Are your parents home?"

"Papa's in his office. I'll see if he can come out," I said as calmly as I could. I was trying to buy time so that I could figure out how to tell them the truth. How did you tell someone your crazy father had locked your drawings up in a closet because at the moment he thought they were real people and would be slaughtered if he let them out in the light of day?

"Papa?"

"Come in," he said, his voice still eerily modulated.

"Papa, these people came to see my drawings and if you don't get them for me. . ." I stopped. In his hands were three rolls of paper.

"Be careful with them. Don't let them out of your sight, but I do think they could use a little sunlight. They've gotten so pale here in the darkness."

The curtains were drawn, but I didn't have time to worry about it right then. I slipped out of the room and found Mr. Paleri and Mrs. Morris in the living room.

"Sorry, Papa's on a deadline, but I do have three of my drawings here."

I opened them slowly, praying they were really mine. I let my breath out as I opened each one and laid it on the floor with books from the shelves to weigh the corners.

The two adults silently stared at my drawings without comment. I felt like crying. "Wait," I cried out.

I retrieved my painting of the cello cases from under my bed where I had stored it and hurried back.

"I have this, too," I said.

Mrs. Morris sat down, her eyes still fixed on my drawings. She transferred her gaze to my painting, still not saying a word.

"It's my first real painting," I apologized. "I mean, I like it, but maybe it isn't very good."

Mrs. Morris cleared her throat. "Sara, these are fine! In fact, they are wonderful! I can see why the judges were taken aback. Where did you come up with these images?"

I swallowed hard. "I see them in my head. Is that okay?"
She threw Mr. Paleri a glance. "Oh yes! That is just fine. Good for you."

Breathe, breathe deeply. You're safe now.

"Well, I'm sorry we missed your parents," Mr. Paleri said.

"It was wonderful meeting you, and getting to see your work was a real treat. I mean that, Sara! Mr. Paleri says he can help you get your slides made if you need him to, but please, please do apply!"

She was almost begging me.

"I will, I promise," I said.

They climbed back in their car. Where was Mama? I could hardly wait to tell her! I faced the door to the study. I should tell Papa. I should return the drawings to him, shouldn't I?

I stood nervously in front of the closed door, unable to decide what to do.

After several minutes, I went outside to sit on the stoop and Willie came out of his house with my back pack and shoes.

"Did you get here in time?" he asked.

"Yeah, barely."

"Was your father home? His car is here."

"Yeah, he's home. He's in his study. Willie," I said quietly. "I think I'm gonna get to study art in New York this summer! Isn't that amazing?"

"Nah, Sara. You deserve it!"

"Thanks. I hope Mama will let me go."

"Aw, your father will make her let you. My father, he'd stop me if I was offered a chance to study cello in New York."

I was tired, so tired, and I rested my head on Willie's shoulder, and he let me. If felt good, and solid, and real.

"Willie, my Papa's sick again. I was really, really scared he'd come out and ruin everything."

"Do you want me to wait with you until your mother gets home?"

"Would you mind?" I asked. "I don't think I wanna be alone in the house."

Alone? Papa was in there with all his friends—his family, the family I had made up in class. In a flash, what I had said came back to me. I had lied, boldly made up an entire family tree for Papa, and everyone on it was from Papa's stories!

Good News

Mama found Willie and me sitting on the stoop when she got home. The sun was almost setting and her hair was wind swept. Willie said good-bye as she walked up, and I threw my arms around her in a giant hug.

"Good heavens, Sara, what's that for?"

I wasn't sure. Was it because of my good news, or because I was relieved that she was home and I didn't have to be alone with Papa? And which should I tell her about first?

What came out was, "Where were you, Mama?"

She brushed at her hair and said, "Sara, we have to talk."

I followed her into the kitchen where she nervously put on a pot of tea. She got out two cups: mine, with the little Peter Rabbit on it and hers, a large, round pottery mug. I waited for her to start, guiltily relieved that I didn't have to make a decision about which news to tell her first.

"What's up, Mama?"

"Where's Papa?"

So it was decided. I had to tell her. I cast my eyes down at my feet and said, "Under the barn floor."

She sat down heavily into a kitchen chair. "I was afraid of that." She laid her head on the table, every movement speaking of utter weariness.

"Mama, what's the matter?"

Her eyes were puffy as if she had been crying, but before she answered, the tea kettle whistled, making me jump.

"Maybe we should see if Papa would like some tea?"

"Yeah, okay, I've got something to return to him anyway."

I retrieved the rolls of drawings from the living room and knocked timidly at the study door. No answer. I cracked the door. Papa wasn't there.

I laid the drawings against a wall and went upstairs. No Papa. "Mama, is Papa with you?"

She came to the foot of the steps and shook her head.

"He must have gone out," I said.

"I guess we should go outside and look for him," Mama said listlessly.

The last lingering rays of sun were all that lit the sky as twilight fell. Mama got the flashlight from under the sink and we walked around the yard. No Papa. The night was almost balmy and I heard the first spring peepers singing over near Small Lake Pond.

It made me want to linger in the yard, but Mama was already on the way inside. By the time I got to the door, she was dialing someone on the phone, but she stopped when I cried out, "Mama! Look! Look!"

There stood Papa in the front hall in all his unkempt glory.

"Where were you, Michel? You frightened us!"

"I took Sara's advice and went walking in the sunshine. "It was so beautiful! I barely made it back by nightfall. Is it fair that the soldiers make us live in darkness?"

"No, it isn't fair," Mama answered. "Why don't you go take a shower before dinner."

"What are you going to bring me tonight?" he asked.

"Tuna fish sandwiches and vegetable soup from a can," I said quickly, knowing that Mama hadn't thought that far ahead.

"Ah! Will you put celery and green peppers and a little apple in the tuna?"

"If you like," Mama said.

He went up towards the bathroom with Mama's eyes following him until she couldn't see him anymore.

"Mama, what did you want to tell me?"

"What? Oh, it can wait, it can wait."

"I got some good news today," I said.

"Really? I could use some good news."

I cleared my throat and announced my nomination proudly.

Mama frowned. Her eyes got misty and suddenly she slammed the plastic bowl in her hand down and ran from the room. I was dismayed. What had I said? What had I done? Why wasn't she happy for me?

I found Mama sitting in the dark in Papa's living room chair, running a finger along the surface of my baby picture.

"Sara, I am very proud of you. Really I am!"

"But you don't want me to go?" I asked. Why was everything so confusing?

"No, no! You should go. It's a wonderful opportunity and you should go."

"Mama, why are you crying? I thought you'd be happy."

"Oh, Sara, I am, I am."

She held her arms out to me as Papa came pounding down the stairs.

"It was good to get all the dirt off," he said. "Thank you for letting me use the shower."

Mama sat up stiffly. "Michel, Sara has good news."

"*Sara?*" He looked perplexed. "Didn't *Sara* die?"

Mama clenched my hand in hers so hard it hurt. "Yes, your sister died."

"But I'm your daughter, Papa!" I said. Mama squeezed harder. "My name is Sara, too."

Papa bowed his head and rubbed at his forehead and under his breath he hummed, "*Thrump. Thrump!*" He looked up. "I have to go back, don't I?" Before we could answer, he walked into the study, looked around and slowly, hesitantly unlocked the closet door and stepped into it. The door shut behind him and I heard him say, "*Thrump, thrumppp.*"

I pressed my ear against the wood of the door. "*Thrump, thrump, thrump.*" I could hear the vibration from within.

"Mama, what are we going to do?" I cried.

"I don't know, Sara. I don't know!"

"Why can't he be okay? How can he change so fast?"

She shook her head. Her lips were trembling. If I left for the summer she would be all alone in the house with Papa. And she was afraid.

"Mama, I'm not going to New York," I said sadly. "I can't leave you."

Her eyes were glossy and I could see she was barely holding back the tears. "Sara, you should go. I'll be all right. I'll take Papa to the doctor tomorrow. Maybe medicine will help him."

I closed my eyes and tried not to sob. I didn't want my Papa drugged into sanity. I wanted him to be real, to know who I was and who Mama was, all the time, but our options were running out.

"If medicine doesn't work, what then?" I asked.

Mama didn't answer.

My legs were so heavy I wasn't sure I could make it up the steps to my room. Dazed and scared, I collapsed on my bed, grabbed up Bear and howled. It wasn't fair! My papa was a good man. My mama deserved to be happy. Suddenly I understood how Nana felt. She liked Papa okay, but she didn't like what he did to Mama. I sat up and sobbed as I stared into tear-blurred space. What happened to people who went mad? Truly and finally mad!

Ivan Watson's Chocolate Bar

Willie stopped by my house on the way to school and we walked together. Butch whizzed by us on his shiny-new red bike with fancy yellow trim and matching duotone red-and-yellow banana seat.

"I really hate that kid!" Willie said. "What're your plans for revenge?"

"Uh, I've been too busy to figure that out," I said.

"Well, I've got a good one."

"Yeah?" My spirits lifted a little bit. I needed something else to think about other than Papa and right then, revenge sounded sweet.

"Yeah! You know that new bike he brags about all the time? Maybe we should just give him a taste of his own medicine."

"What'd you have in mind, Willie? Just spill it!"

"We could sneak out during school and, uh, add a little bit of decoration to it. Like a mustache or two?"

A smile spread across my face, a big smile that got bigger by the minute. "You are a genius, Willie Jensen. Brilliant!"

He started to whistle and his fingers slipped into mine as we walked along.

We met after school and went to the hardware store. "What color, Willie?"

"Purple," Willie said, "to match the ink on your drawing. Ironic justice, wouldn't you say?"

We chose a small can and two small brushes, took it to the counter, and Willie paid the three dollars and fifty-five cents they cost. We practically ran home.

"I gotta cello lesson, but tonight I'll come over to do our homework and we can plan then. I don't want Harriet listening in, so it's gotta be at your house."

"Sure," I said, "I'll see you then."

I whistled a little tune that faded the minute I stepped over the threshold to my house. A dreary haze hung inside, as if my father left a trail wherever he passed.

"Mama, is Papa here?"

She shook her head, and dried her hands on the kitchen towel. "He went to a meeting."

"What? He's okay?"

"I don't know, Sara. He said he had an important client and that he couldn't wait any longer."

"What'd that mean?"

She shrugged. "Mr. Paleri called with the name of a photographer to get your slides made. What pieces are you going to submit?"

"I don't know. I guess I'll have to ask Papa to get out all my drawings."

"I have the key. Do you want to get them out now, Sara?"

"I don't know. I think we should ask Papa to help. Maybe today, while he's well."

We ate dinner without Papa. He had told Mama he'd be late. It began to rain and soon thunder was rumbling through the sky. I saw lightning split the night outside, but still no Papa.

Mama walked up and down the room, across and back.

"Mama, stop," I begged.

"Your grandfather used to say I could wear a path in a rug with my pacing. Sara, maybe I should call the police. He's very late!"

"Maybe he's waiting out the storm," I suggested as the lights went out.

"I'll get the flashlight," Mama said. Lightning lit the room and I saw her with her hands out, feeling about.

Just then the front door burst open, and Papa stood there. He pulled off his hat and shook it by, sending droplets flying. He hung it on the doorknob and pulled off his suit jacket. "Here, Sara, come take this. It's soaking wet."

I held it away from me and watched the coat drip puddles onto the floor. "The lights are out, Papa."

"I see that."

Mama came in with a candle, the flame-light catching her face, making her look ghostly. Papa jerked. "You startled me, Lea."

"I'm sorry. The batteries died in the flashlight. How was your meeting?"

"Long. Late."

"Papa, can I get my drawings so a man can take slides of them?" I asked spontaneously, suddenly dying to tell him about what had happened.

"What for, Sara? The slides, I mean."

"Oh, Michel, Sara has been chosen to apply for a summer course in New York, all paid for, too! Isn't that wonderful?"

"Ah! So it all worked out. Good for you, my sweet Sara."

He called me that when he was proud and I usually beamed, but this time I couldn't quite forget that Mama would be alone in the house with the Michel who, for parts of his life, still lived deep in a hole, under a barn.

"I'll get you some coffee," Mama said to him.

Papa went upstairs, and after a few minutes I followed him. He had already slipped into a warm sweater and was pulling on dry socks.

"Are you cold?" I asked.

"Yes. It's very wet out. So you might go to New York?"

"I'm thinking about it. It depends on lots of things."

"What things, Sara?" he asked. The storm lit his face in brief bursts of lightning which disappeared quickly, only to illuminate us again a few minutes later.

"Well, if I'm accepted, that's the first thing. And then, there's the thing if you think it's a good program. And then, there's the thing about Mama."

"What about Mama?"

I thought, breathe, breathe, now say it! "Mama doesn't want me to leave her."

"But I'll be here," Papa said.

I couldn't look at him as I said, "Sometimes you're here, but sometimes you're in the hole. Do you remember when you're in the hole?"

I saw him cringe. Then he hung his head and said, "Sometimes the hole is so real. I hear everybody calling to me to come back and rescue them. What should I do, leave them there to starve?"

"Papa, were any of them real? I mean any of the people who came to your hiding place?"

I couldn't describe the look in his eyes, the emotions that rolled across his face as I asked him that. He whispered, his voice so low I could barely hear it. "I am not sure, Sara. I am not sure anymore."

I patted his back. "I bet the coffee is ready. It'll warm you up. I gotta call Willie and see if he wants to do our work by candlelight. We're sharing a project," I said.

Papa pulled a comb from his pocket and ran it through his hair while I called Willie, who said he'd be right over and thanked me for an excuse to get away from Harriet, who had been talking incessantly on the phone until their mother had made her take an hour's break. I had barely hung up before he stood on our porch with a dripping umbrella hanging over his head.

"Hey, Sara. Am I fast or what?"

"Anything to get away from Harriet?"

"Yep, anything, even the dreaded Sara Goldman's house!" He broke into a grin as he said it, and at that exact moment, the lights magically stuttered and came back on.

"Hi, Willie," Papa said as he came out of the kitchen with a cup of coffee in his hand.

"Papa, where can we work?"

"Well, since the electricity has come back on, Mama and I are going to watch the television. I'll tell you what, you and Willie can work in my study."

"Cool!" Willie said.

I wasn't so sure, but then again, it meant Papa wouldn't be in there. It seemed it was when he was in the study that he transformed. Maybe I should keep records, should try and trace what set off the changes.

"So," Willie said, interrupting my chain of thought, "your father seems okay."

"Yeah, for now."

"Can you sketch a mustache so I'll have something to copy?"

"Oh, come on, Willie! You gotta be kidding. Anyone can draw a handlebar mustache!"

"No, not anyone! I can't. I tried at home. I guess you gotta give Butch credit for that, don't you? He can draw a mustache!"

"I'm not giving him credit for anything."

Willie stood over me while I drew at Papa's desk. His hand brushed mine as he pointed at what I was doing, and I was surprised to feel a little thrill go through me. It was silly. I'd known Willie my whole life. I concentrated on my drawing, which didn't take long.

"Will that do?"

"Uh huh. You know, Sara, I was thinking, if you want, I could sit for you and you could draw me, and maybe if it was any good, you could send it off to New York."

"Huh? I thought you never wanted anyone to take your picture, and now you want me to draw your portrait?"

"That was before I became the new, thinner me, don't you think?" he asked, prancing around with his hand up to his face above a silly grin. "That's an imitation of Harriet," he added.

He was right, he was growing and he was getting thinner, and I hadn't noticed.

"And besides, if you draw me, it's about the only way I'm gonna get to New York."

"Sure, why not? We can start now."

I chose a medium-sized sheet of paper from Papa's flat files and a small drawing board. "Here," I said, pulling out a chair. "Sit there."

"Uh, why am I in the middle of the room?"

"Shsssh. Just stare at one place and stay perfectly still."

I walked around him, looking for the best position.

"Sara, why are you walking around me?"

"Shsssh, just let me look at you."

"This is spooky."

"Willie, be quiet! Artists have to concentrate."

"Oh, okay," he said and shut up.

I had never really thought of Willie as handsome. I'd never really thought of him as anything much except my friend. But as I stared at him, I saw him differently. His pudginess was disappearing into developing lines. His eyes dominated his face and he had a high, clear forehead. His cheekbones were emerging from baby chub and his ears lay flat against his head in precisely the way ears were supposed to, but rarely did. I drew the way Papa had taught me when we went sketching. I drew without looking down much. I stared at my subject to see him clearly, which was good, because otherwise I would have drawn the Willie I had always known, instead of the emerging man before me. I hoped my smile didn't show on my face, but I could feel it spread inside of me as I thought of Willie as a man.

Willie broke out in a hum, which quickly shifted to a question. "Any requests? I mean, I can't just sit here and not even talk, so I'll sing if you want."

"Willie, just a few more minutes."

"I gotta ask you something that's been bothering me, Sara."

I stopped drawing. "Okay, what is it? But then you gotta be still a little longer!"

"What are you gonna do about what you said in history?"

"Now you broke my concentration! I don't wanna talk about that right now. Just sit still for a little longer."

"Sorry, but don't snap my head off!"

Willie was right. He was my friend and it wasn't his fault. "I'm sorry," I said sheepishly.

"Can I come in?" Papa asked from the hall. He walked over to where I sat and looked down. "Very nice, Sara, but I don't think you can finish tonight. It's late and you two have school tomorrow."

"Yes, sure, you're right, Papa. I'll clean up."

"So, Willie, come see the plans for your music room."

"I thought my dad nixed it."

"Not that I have heard yet. Let me show you what I've designed."

Papa pulled out a sheet of vellum. He spread it out on the drafting table and turned on the swing arm lamp that sat there.

"It has a lovely tile floor, I think with a pinkish tone to it."

"Mr. Goldman, this is a round room!"

"Octagonal, actually. I thought you could line some of the walls in bookcases and some with floor-to-ceiling built-in sheet music cabinets. If I do this room correctly, it will act as a natural microphone when you sit and practice in the center of it."

"Wow! Oh, wow!" Willie exclaimed. "But, Mr. Goldman, my dad is never going to pay for something this fancy."

"No, Willie, he probably won't build it."

"Yeah," Willie said dejectedly, "and you will have wasted your time."

Papa patted Willie's arm and said, "No, I won't have wasted my time. This is a gift to you, Willie. If your father doesn't build it, then when you are a famous cellist you can use the design yourself!"

"Really?"

Papa nodded.

"You really think I can be a famous cellist, Mr. Goldman?"

Papa nodded again. "Absolutely, Willie. And Sara, you will be a famous artist. Now home with you, Willie. You'll have to come back so Sara can finish the drawing, okay?"

"Sure, sure. Thanks, Sara! Thanks, Mr. Goldman!"

I saw Willie to the door and came back to Papa, who was putting the plans for Willie's music room away. I kissed his cheek and was about to leave when he said, "Sara, I want to tell you a story."

"Now, Papa?" Oh, how I didn't want a story.

"Yes. It's because of the question you asked me, about who was real and who wasn't."

"Can we talk in another room?" I asked hopefully, thinking again about Papa's transformations in this room.

"Yes, sure. I think maybe Mama should hear this, too."

"She doesn't like your stories, Papa."

"I know, but this time she needs to listen. While I can, I want to try to explain."

We walked back into the living room and I sat, balancing uneasily on the edge of the sofa while Papa went to get Mama.

"What is it, Michel?" she asked.

"Come, Lea, I need you to listen, even if you don't want to. I want to tell you a story."

"Now, Michel?"

"Sit, Lea. Listen. Then we can all go to bed."

She reluctantly sank into the pillows next to me, her arms crossed as if she could keep herself out of it by taking that stance.

"All right. Sara asked me if anyone in the hole, anyone I talk about was real. The truth is, after two years, I couldn't remember who was real and who wasn't. I was ten when I started hiding. Ten! Little more than a baby. Before the war, I had been a chubby little boy, not very tall for my age. When I came out of hiding, I was a skeletal child who had grown not even a fraction of an inch. Not only did I not know who was real while I lived beneath the floor, I also could not tell how much time elapsed between one visit from the farmer to the next. It was as if the whole world had ceased to acknowledge my existence. I began to forget my family. The only images of them I could call up were of their deaths. Everything else lay hidden outside of my life."

Mama's body relaxed and she reached for my hand. Papa's eyes were fixed on the dark windows still lit sporadically by the fiery electric storm.

"Maybe everybody was make-believe," I said.

"No, not everyone. That was what made it so hard. One time the farmer pulled the floor back and said, 'Michel, someone needs to hide with you.' I wasn't prepared for who slid into the hole. It was an adult. He took up a lot of space as he dropped a bulky pack in front of him. I wondered if there was enough air for the two of us. I wondered if there would be enough food. It had gotten very meager in the last few days.

"The man rummaged around in the pack and pulled out a big flashlight. The bulb appeared like brilliant sunlight to me when he turned it on, and it took a long time for my eyes to adjust and even then, there was a hazy glow around everything. This man spoke with a funny accent that convinced me he was from far away.

"'You hungry?' he asked.

"Yes, I was hungry, I was always hungry, but I didn't answer him. I actually wondered if he was real or if I was imagining him. That's funny, isn't it? But no grown-up had ever hidden with me before. I had not seen an adult, except for the farmer, since I had found my mother and father lying on our floor.

"'Want a chocolate bar or some C-rations? It's all I got, but there's plenty for two.'

"My mouth watered for that candy bar, but my tongue wouldn't form words. It had been too long since I had used it.

"'What's your name?' He was trying so hard. When I think about it now, I feel badly that I never answered him. But I couldn't, I really couldn't! Before long, I was afraid that if I spoke to him, he would disappear.

"'What's your name? Mine's Ivan Watson.'

"Even though I didn't speak a word to Ivan Watson the whole time he shared my hiding place, it didn't matter. He talked for both of us.

"'So how long you been down here?' He looked at a silver wrist watch with a large face on it. 'I've got twenty-four hours to wait here. Hope I'm not scaring you. My mother came from New Orleans, had some French in her, and she always said my accent was horrible. Can you even understand me?'

"Ivan Watson was a big man, tall with wide shoulders and dark skin. 'You ever seen a Negro before, kid? Nope, probably not. Why're you hiding? Me, I got left behind. Well, sorta. My plane came down. Course, I came down separately in a parachute. Right in the farmer's field. Real piece of luck, that!'

"Ivan handed me the chocolate. 'My boy back home, he loves candy. Wanna see a picture of him?' He pulled out a crinkled photograph. A woman with a boy of maybe eleven or twelve years stared at me. They were all dressed up, the boy in a suit, with a little bow tie and the woman in a striped dress. "Pretty when she's gussied up," Ivan Watson said longingly and touched his wife's face. 'We're planning on a bunch of kids when I get back.' He kissed the picture and touched his wife's tiny face again.

"I reached out and touched the face of his watch. It was one o'clock. One o'clock in the morning or night? I had no idea.

"'You don't have a clock, do you, boy?' He shone the flashlight around the hole. 'Man, this place is small. That bear the only thing you got down here to play with?' He didn't even have to move to reach across the space and pick up poor Bear. I grabbed her from him almost snarling, although I remember being surprised at the sound in my throat.

"'How long you been down here, child?' he asked.

"I wanted to tell him, except I didn't know. How long? What day, what year was it? None of my other cellmates had ever asked me that. How long?

"After a while, even Ivan quit talking. He turned the flashlight off and once in a while, I heard him gently snoring. Then his body would spasm for a second, his eyes would flutter and he would check his watch with the flashlight. I sat up the whole time watching him. I suppose it must have been nighttime, but the hour of a day had ceased to mean anything to me long ago. Finally, he turned on the light, stretched, looked at his watch, stretched again, his long arms raised and pointing upwards.

"'Listen, boy, I'm gonna be going soon, so I'll leave you some stuff.' He made a stack of candy, canned goods and a can opener. 'You need it more 'n me.' He pushed the pile over in my direction. 'I got about fifteen minutes and then I'm leaving. You stay safe now, you hear?'

"The hands of his wristwatch moved, counting off my minutes with Ivan Watson. He stood up and looked above him, then stopped. 'Listen here, you take care of my picture, okay?' he asked, handing me the little photograph. 'And when this is over, you come see me if you can get to the U.S. of A. My address is on the back of that photo. And here!' He took off the watch and gave it to me. I hope I said thank you or all right, but I don't remember it. I have wondered about that for many years.

"Pretty soon the floor above our heads slid aside, someone threw a rope down and Ivan pulled himself up. Then the floor was back in place and he was gone, but the stack of food sat on the dirt next to Bear. I held the watch in my hands, feeling the hard, cold steel and pushed it up my arm, almost to my shoulder before it fit. I watched the hands move and listened to it tick. My own father had had a pocket watch. The minute my father came to mind, I pushed the thought away. I picked up Bear and held her tightly. And then I heard gunfire and I jerked, as if I had been struck. I knew Ivan Watson's boy would never see him. I knew Ivan Watson's boy would never hear his father's voice again. I knew I had been the last person alive to see Ivan Watson in the light."

Papa stood and stretched, with the same gesture I had just imagined Ivan had used right before he left. Papa blinked, brought his arms down and pulled an envelope from his pocket. In it was a chocolate bar wrapper and a crumpled photo. "The watch, I still wear," he said holding out his hand, pulling his shirt from the wrist.

"You know, when Ivan Watson left was the moment I went mad. Until that moment, I had believed with surety that all my friends were real. But when he gave me the watch, when I felt the cold metal in my hand marking real time, in that moment I found doubt. And in the doubt, I found guilt. Guilt that I questioned the benevolence of my friends. While the watch ticked I woke from sleep to question who was dream and who was real. Did the farmer hide me to save me or torture me? I waited for the light that the timepiece promised, but it never dawned. Days passed like that and then I over-wound the watch, the ticking stopped, and its hands no longer moved. Time started to stretch out into darkness again. The farmer failed to come for a long, long time. I was alone and soon the Trickster came. Ivan Watson was dead, but the Trickster, he was there and I welcomed him."

Mama shook her head, and stood up. "Michel, Sara and I are real. We're here now, and we need you."

"Yes, yes. I know, but what if I am the only person who remembers any of them; if the only way their lives are real, is in my memory? How can I let them go?"

"No, Michel! Enough! No *buts* allowed," Mama said, and stomped off.

Papa said to me, "You understand, don't you, Sara?"

"Papa, you have to make a choice," I said.

"I must talk to Mama," was his answer. He put the envelope in my hand and left the room.

I pulled out the crumpled picture of the woman and the boy in their Sunday best smiling at the camera that had snapped their portrait. Poor Papa.

Operation Mustache

Morning came and I had barely slept. Mama and Papa had argued all night. Papa's voice had sounded as if he was in agony, Mama's like she was crying. When I did fall asleep, Ivan Watson visited my dreams and when I woke in the morning, I pocketed the photograph to take to school with me.

Willie walked out of his house as I walked out of mine. He had a brown bag with the paint and the brushes in it. The mustache sketch was folded up in his back pocket.

"I still can't believe you need my sketch!"

"Believe it, I need it! So, I got my mom to write me a note to get me out of P.E. I told her I twisted my ankle."

"You lied?" I asked.

"It's for a good cause, and besides, we're doing wrestling and I hate wrestling. Yesterday Larry broke a thumb during wrestling, Sara."

I nodded. Thumbs were important to cellists.

"So, I'm gonna take care of business. Besides, Butch'll never think of me as the culprit. See ya," he said as we got to school.

Mr. Paleri grinned at me as I came in. I looked around for Butch, but he wasn't there. My stomach did somersaults until he slipped in just before the bell rang. I pulled out the photograph and began a drawing. I sketched in the picture of Ivan I held in my mind and then overlaid it with the child and the woman. Ivan was huge, and I shaded him in pale, soft grays. A shadow. A ghost in their lives. A ghost in my Papa's. Then I added another figure. Small, skinny with a big watch pushed up his arm, holding hands with Ivan's boy, my Papa was ghostly gray where he touched Ivan's son, and just on the other edge, became sharp and real. I worked so hard I barely noticed Mr. Paleri stop and look over my shoulder and move on. I didn't see Amy watching me as I drew. I looked up only to grab a few colored pencils to fill in the boy and his mother with light color and then a little more, until they stood crisply in the front.

When I looked up everyone else was gone. The bell had rung and I hadn't heard it. There was no second period in the art room so I was all alone. I looked at the clock and remembered it hadn't worked in days. I had no idea what time it was, or where I was supposed to be, or why Mr. Paleri hadn't kicked me out.

Just like your father. Time has gone on without you, Lovely Lili's voice reprimanded me.

It had to be before third period. If it was third period, other kids would be streaming in. I'd missed Science. I hadn't meant to cut, but here I was, still working in Art. I picked up my drawing, covered it in a slip-sheet of blank paper and rolled it carefully. I tucked it under my arm and waited. Almost immediately the bell rang and I walked into the hall. The kids consumed the passageway and I headed into what I hoped was third period.

Amy grabbed my arm. "Where were you?"

"In Art. I didn't hear the bell. What'd I miss? Did Miss Palmer notice I wasn't there?"

"Not really. We had a sub, and I said present twice when you didn't show up."

"Thanks, Amy!"

"Is that the drawing you were doing?"

"Yeah."

"Can I see it later?"

"Sure."

"Hey, Sara, you do remember there's an assembly now, don't you?" Amy asked.

"Huh, no, I forgot. What's it about?"

"I don't know. They called it first period."

"We walked to the gym where they always held assemblies and climbed into the bleachers. I saw Willie high up, and Amy and I climbed up to sit next to him.

"So?" I whispered.

"Done," he whispered back. "Two, one on each fender, but I don't know how good they are. Wasn't much room for them."

"Hey, you two, don't whisper when I'm here," Amy said, sticking me with an elbow.

"Sorry," I said.

The principal stood up. "Ladies and Gentlemen, we are very pleased to have the unexpected opportunity to present the Harlem Globetrotters!" A great cheer went up from the boys, while the girls slumped on the bleachers.

"They're cool, wait and see," Willie said to me and Amy.

Out ran these super tall, wiry, muscled men in their shorts and sleeveless, shiny red-white-and-blue uniforms. The first one stepped out and spun the ball on one finger. It dizzied around until he tossed it to another. Back and forth they went from one trick to the next. Impossible shots from beneath their legs, incredible pass-offs and fancy maneuverings. Maybe everyone around me was in awe of the skill and prowess of these guys, but to me they were dancers and what did I do, but see another painting. Unfortunately, I didn't have paper to draw them and doubted I could keep such complex positions in my mind's eye, but I watched in fascination.

"Wish I could draw that," I mumbled.

Willie leaned over and said, "You don't have to draw every-thing. Relax and enjoy it, Sara."

He took my hand in his and I smiled. It was nice being a little more than friends with Willie. Amy nudged me and grinned knowingly.

The rest of the day passed in a school haze until history. Last period, I thought as I slipped into my chair. I sat up straight all of a sudden. Our final projects were due today, and mine was at home in my desk drawer.

Mrs. Bancroft fixed her eye on me as soon as I came in. I slouched into my seat. "Sara, could I see you for a moment?"

I came forward. "It's come to my attention," she said as quietly as she could, "that you may need extra time for your project. Mr. Paleri has told me you have something important to take care of, so I'm giving you an extension until the end of next week.

"Gee, thanks, Mrs. Bancroft!"

"One more thing, Sara. Please be sure to verify all your facts when you write your report." She gave me a crooked smile.

I sank back into my chair, resting my head on my desk for a minute. The horrible, dreaded Mrs. Bancroft had just given me a way out! I couldn't believe it. I sat up and looked right at her and when she glanced my way, I smiled at her. She deserved it. And she smiled back.

Willie and I left the building hand-in-hand. He whistled a classical melody and I basked in having my first boyfriend. We were passing the bike racks when we saw Butch coming to unlock his bike.

"Keep moving, Willie."

"Don't worry," he said.

We were twenty feet past him when Butch's howl filled the air. "Who did this? Who did this?" We looked over our shoulders. He was turning in circles screaming into the air. Then he saw us. "Sara Goldman!" he screeched and ran at us.

We stood our ground to meet him.

"You did this!" he snarled, as Willie stepped between him and me.

Butch wasn't much taller than Willie anymore and Willie had fifteen pounds on him. I saw Butch take a step back, re-evaluating this new version of Willie.

"What'd she do, Butch?" Willie asked with perfectly feigned innocence.

"Painted something on my new bike!"

"Yeah? What?" Willie asked.

"I'm not sure what! Something curly and girly," Butch yowled.

A crowd was gathering. The boys were watching with lit up eyes and the girls were nervously shifting their weight from foot to foot.

"Why would she do that?" Willie asked.

"She knows why!" Butch almost spit he was so mad. A deep scarlet was creeping up his neck towards his cheeks.

"I do? I don't have any idea why you'd think that," I said.

"Revenge," he said angrily.

"Why would she want revenge on you, unless you're the one who ruined her drawing?" Amy chimed in helpfully from out of the crowd. "Did you do that, Butch?"

He looked around frantically, trying to think of a way out. "No! I'd never do that."

"Then why would you think Sara would do something to your bike?" Willie demanded, putting his hands on his hips stubbornly.

Butch stuck his face an inch from mine. "You did this, didn't you? Admit it!"

I gathered my words and said honestly, "I didn't touch your bike, Butch."

"I'm gonna get you good, Sara Goldman," he snarled.

"Whatcha gonna do, Butch, beat a girl up?" one of the boys called out.

Everyone waited. Butch looked around again, clenching his fists over and over before he shoved and pushed through the crowd back towards his bike.

One of the teachers saw the gathering and came up, saying, "Break it up, break it up! No loitering."

It was over. Willie and I walked on our way, waving to Amy. When we turned down our own block, smiles spread across our faces and we burst into laughter.

"We did it," Willie said. "The fat boy and the weird girl got Butch!"

"Yeah," I said and kissed his cheek. He looked at me, feeling where I had touched him with his fingertips.

Then he took my hand and held it all the way to my door.

Thirty-Five William Watsons

Mama met us at the door and our hands flew apart.

"I need to tell you something," she said without commenting on our hand-holding. I remembered she had wanted to tell me something before.

"Sure. Bye, Willie." He waved and trotted to his house.

Mama stood right where she was, looked around as if seeking an escape before she finally came out with, "Sara, well, you're, well, you're going to have a baby sister or brother!"

"What?" I looked at Mama and she nodded. "Really? Oh boy!" I cried and grabbed her and hugged her. "That's great!"

"Around Thanksgiving," she said.

"Does Papa know? What'd he say?"

She shook her head. "Not yet. That's what I really need to talk to you about. Sara, we can't go on like this. Papa's stories are getting to be more and more realistic. I'm afraid they're taking over."

"But, Mama, maybe Papa's story about Ivan Watson is true. I've never heard that one before. Couldn't it be a sign that he's separating what was real from what wasn't?" I asked hopefully.

"Oh, I wish that was so, but Papa collects old pictures, Sara. People he's never seen or known! He has a whole box full of them, all with names on the back. Until the other night, I thought it was a harmless obsession. But now, he's adding them to his stories!" She sucked in her breath and said, "The doctor wants to put Papa in a hospital for a while."

"No! No, Mama! You can't do that. Papa's not crazy!"

She gave me a look and said with her voice close to breaking, "I think he may be, Sara."

"No," I screamed, "no! You can't do this. It'll kill him!"

She backed away from me before she said, "What else can I do? Maybe he'll be back by the time the baby is born."

"No, Mama! It's wrong! If you send him away, he'll never come back, not ever! I know it!"

"I'm sorry, Sara. I'm going to make the arrangements by the end of the week." She stepped away from me, avoiding my eyes, and said, "I'm going into town. Do you want to come?"

"No!" I yelled at her. "I don't ever wanna to talk to you again! Not ever!"

As the front door slammed behind her, I dumped my backpack and collapsed on the floor next to it. Anger engulfed me and I kicked the pack into the wall and screamed until I was out of breath. Drained, I found myself staring at the drawing of Ivan Watson and his family unrolling itself on the floor as the tape hinge on it gave way. The photograph lay in the middle of it where I had left it. I picked it up and turned it over. *Eva and Billy Watson* was labeled on the back.

In a daze I thought, Billy, William, right? He'd be Papa's age, wouldn't he? How old would Eva be? Nana's age? Younger? Older? I felt my mind clearing and fingered the letters of the address. Could they still live at the same place in New York

City? I heaved myself off the floor, walked slowly into Papa's study and closed the door. I looked at the phone and dialed the *zero* for the operator.

"I want the telephone number for William or Eva Watson in New York City," I said.

"I have thirty-five William Watsons, but no Evas," the calm voice responded.

I read the address off. "I'm sorry, no one at that address. Would you like any of the phone numbers?"

"Sure," I replied. "All thirty-five."

"All of them?"

"Yes, and their addresses."

"I'm sorry, we don't give out addresses," she said. "Are you ready for the listings?"

By the time I was finished, my hand was cramped. My writing had gotten progressively sloppier, but there sat thirty-five William Watsons, and I had no idea if any of them was the right one. If I could prove to Mama that Ivan Watson had been real, maybe she would reconsider committing Papa, but I knew she didn't want to hope any more and would stop me if she caught me calling. I needed help.

I called Nana. "Nana, I need your help!"

"With what, sweetie?" she asked.

"I need to use your phone to make a lot of phone calls."

"Sara, what on earth for?"

"I gotta find someone in New York City. I just gotta!"

There was no answer on the other end until she said, "Why, Sara? You'll have to tell me why."

"To save Papa," I wept.

"Don't cry. I'll be right over to pick you up. Now, hush, hush. I'm coming."

There was a click. I sat down and waited, sniffling every once in a while. I heard Nana's car pull up, grabbed the photograph and the list of numbers and dashed outside.

She drove slowly. "Do you want to stop for a snack?"

"No, we gotta hurry."

"Sara, is this because your mother wants to commit your father?"

My eyes narrowed. "Was that your idea?" I asked.

"No, but I can't say it's wrong."

"It's wrong, Nana! It means Papa will end. He won't ever build another building. He won't ever get to make Willie's music room for him. Nana, I need Papa!"

I saw tears in her eyes. "Okay, right home we go. You can call, but what do you think it'll prove?"

"That some of Papa's people were real; that he is beginning to be able to tell the difference."

Her lips parted and then she clamped them together, but when we pulled up she didn't get right out of the car.

"Sara," she said, "I don't know if finding someone who was real is enough. Your father is very sick. He doesn't always know who you or your mother are. Do you understand?"

"He's never, ever hurt anyone, has he, Nana?" I asked her defensively.

Nana's head moved ever so slightly from side to side. "Sara, he hurts your mother every time he goes back to that hole in the ground. He isn't mean. He isn't a cruel man. He can't help it, but it isn't harmless. And one day, well, who knows?"

"So the war is over, but it still gets to take another victim because we don't believe in Papa?"

Nana's mouth hung open. We got out of the car, neither of us speaking to the other. She showed me into her library room, closed the door and left me facing the phone. I dialed and I dialed. My fingers cramped again and I wiggled them.

"Here, darling," Nana said, coming in with milk and cookies. "Let me try for a while. William Watson?"

"Yes, and his father was Ivan Watson."

She dialed. I watched her manicured nails spin the rotary. I watched her red lips open and close. I munched on a cookie and swallowed, and all the while, I thought of my father: a little boy, emaciated, damaged, trying for his entire life to climb from a hole beneath a barn where he had been buried alive. What would I have done? Could I have survived?

Nana put the phone down. "There are fifteen more numbers, Sara. I don't know if we can finish right now."

"We have to, Nana! Papa survived so much. You and Mama can't give up on him now!"

She picked the phone up again. "I'm calling your mother to tell her you're here before she gets worried."

"I'm going to the bathroom," I said and hurried out.

When I came back, Nana was dialing yet another William Watson number. "Hello, yes, is this William Watson? Yes? Well, I was wondering if your father was Ivan Watson. What? He was?"

I grabbed the phone. "Hi, my name is Sara Goldman. Was your father in the war?"

The voice on the other end was thick and sonorous. Yes, his father had died in the war.

"Really? He did? Oh my God, I found you!"

"Hey, is this a prank?" the voice asked.

"No, no. No prank! My Papa met your father. He saved a picture of you that your father gave him a long time ago."

There was absolute silence on the other end. Then I heard him call to someone. The next person who spoke was a woman whose voice shook as she asked, "Who is this?"

"I have a picture of you and Billy. Your name is Eva and in the picture, you're in a striped dress and Billy has on a bow tie. Ivan carried the picture until just before he died."

I heard her crying. Her son took the phone back and said, "Can I have your phone number? We need to call you back."

"Uh, yeah, but could you call my Papa?"

"Yes, I'd like that. What's his name?" I gave Billy Watson our phone number. I told him Papa's name. I hung up and grabbed Nana and danced around the room with her. When we stopped we were panting and smiling.

Then Nana said, "Now don't get your hopes up too high."

"It's a place to start," I said.

"Yes, perhaps it is. Let's get you home now."

"Mama, Papa!" I screamed as I ran inside. "Mama, Papa, come here!"

Mama was wiping off her hands, her eyebrows knotting into a frown as she hurried from the kitchen. Papa came flying down the stairs.

"What's the matter, Sara?" he asked.

"I found Ivan Watson's son Billy and his wife Eva!"

"Wha, what?" he stammered.

"You found them, Sara? How?" Mama asked in dismay.

"Nana and I called all the William Watson's in the New York phone book and we found him! Billy's gonna call Papa here! Tonight! Isn't it wonderful, Papa? Isn't it, Mama? Ivan Watson was real. Papa, he was real!"

"Is he dead?" Papa asked bluntly.

It wasn't the reaction I had expected. "Yes, Papa."

"Too bad, he was a good man." Papa's hands were shaking as he said it.

Mama clasped his hands between hers as he closed his eyes and leaned his head back. I saw him swallow, over and over.

"I thought you'd be happy to know he was real!" I said, perplexed and confused.

"Well, I'm glad to know it," Nana said.

"Yes, me, too!" Mama added.

Papa rubbed his forehead. "I'm going to lie down."

He ascended the stairs, half bent-over like an old, old man carrying a load.

"I don't understand. I thought Papa would be happy."

Mama rose and followed Papa, her head bowed. She looked back for a moment and gave me a wistful smile.

"What just happened? What'd I do wrong, Nana?"

"This is very complicated, Sara, but I have a question for you," Nana said. "Do you think if you sat down with your father, you could help him figure out which of the people who hid under that barn with him were real, and which of them he made up?"

"I don't know, Nana. What good would that do?"

"Well, maybe, and I don't know if it'd work, but maybe if he knew, he could begin to heal."

"You mean get well?"

"No, I mean heal. You see, Sara, it's as if your father has a big hole in his chest where someone tore a part of him out, and it just won't close up. I think he's afraid to be all alone with all that pain."

"But Mama and I are here. And you."

"Yes, but if he admits to himself that he made up almost everyone he knew while he was in that awful pit, then he has to face such a great loneliness, don't you think?"

It made sense, but I knew from experience that when it came to Papa things didn't always follow a logical pattern.

"Does that mean he has to give up his stories? 'Cause I don't think he can."

Nana thought a moment. "No, I think it means he has to know them for what they are. Stories. Make-believe."

"You mean, he has to put them in the past, like the stories you told to me?"

"That would do, too, yes! I'm going to say good-bye to your mother and then I'm leaving. I love you, Sara."

Nana kissed me good-bye before she left. As I watched her drive off, I pondered what she had said. At last, I put the idea away and was just starting my homework in the living room when someone pounded on our door.

"I'll answer it," Papa called, as he came slowly down the steps. He opened the door and there stood Butch and his father.

"I got a bone to pick with you, Goldman."

"Pardon me?" Papa said.

"Your daughter defaced my son's bike."

Papa's head swung around and he beckoned me forward.

"Did you do that, Sara?"

"I didn't touch his bike, but Butch *is* the one who drew on Lovely Lili!"

"Is that true, Butch?" Papa asked.

That dumb boy could hardly suppress his smirk. "Yeah, well, so what? It wasn't worth anything anyway!"

I saw something in Papa's face change. "You don't think so, do you?"

"Like my boy said, it was just a drawing by a kid."

"Could you and Butch wait here for a moment, Tom?" Papa asked.

Butch's father grumbled out an okay, but irritably muttered and put his hands in and out of his pockets while Papa was gone.

I stared at Butch until he said, "Quit looking at me, weirdo!"

"This is my house and I can look at you if I want to!" I snapped back at him.

I heard Papa coming back, his footfalls heavy on the staircase, but instead of rejoining us immediately in the front hall, I heard him open the study door. He came back out with Lovely Lili in his hands, took some tape and carefully put her up on the hall wall.

"I want her to witness this," he said to us.

He ducked briefly back into the study and reappeared. Dangling in his fingers was the big, black gun from his closet.

"You know," he said in a barely perceptible voice, "my mother and father were killed with this gun. And my little sisters."

"You're crazy! Put that thing away," Butch's father said loudly, but I could see panic in his eyes.

"This drawing Sara did for me, it was of a child named *Lili*, lovely *Lili*. She was seven-and-one-half years old when she stayed with me a few days, and then someone tried to smuggle her out of the country. I never found out if *Lili* survived. Probably not. Ivan Watson, he is dead. And little *Hymen Levi*, he is dead, too."

Butch snickered dumbly and, as if it was a joke, repeated, "Hymen Levi?"

"So you think the name is funny? Yes?"

Papa absently twisted the gun in his hands so that when its barrel steadied, it was pointed just below Butch's waist. Butch crossed his legs as if that would protect him.

"Butch is a pretty funny name, is it not? Do you think someone should shoot you because your name is Butch?" Papa asked, his head cocked to the side.

"My real name is Bertram," Butch declared, as if to make sure Papa wouldn't shoot him over a funny name.

It flitted across my addled mind that Bertram was funnier than Butch. Bertie, I thought, just as Papa asked, "Yes? So, because your name is Bertram, does that mean you are more special than a boy named *Hymen Levi?*"

Butch tried to slip behind his father who was clearly appraising whether he could take Papa.

"You're just as crazy as everyone says you are, Goldman!" Butch's dad burst out.

"Maybe. Sometimes I'm crazier than others, but right now I am just very angry, Tom." It was scary because Papa's voice was syrupy when he spoke.

Mama came out of the kitchen, her eyes widening at the scene. "Michel! What are you doing with that?" she cried out.

"I am explaining to Butch and his father about loss. Butch thinks that his bike is more important than Sara's drawing. But you see, the bike, you will get too big for it, Bertram. It will rust and you will throw it away at the town dump. But this drawing—" He waved the gun at it. "Which will survive longer? Your bicycle or it?"

"I don't know," Butch whined.

His dad was inching towards the door. "Are you leaving? Did I say either of you could leave?" Papa asked.

Butch's father froze, but in that minute, in that instant of a second, Papa pointed the gun at the ceiling and pulled the trigger. I squeezed my eyes shut and winced.

Click!

"It is empty," Papa said. "The only time it was loaded was when the soldiers pulled its trigger and shot my whole family."

Papa was starting to sweat. I could see the strain in his face and so could everyone else. Butch and his dad were shaking. Butch had bitten into his lip and blood dripped from it. A wet spot was on his pants.

His father started to say, "I'll sue, no, I'll call the police, you'll..." He spluttered into silence as Papa's face crumpled.

"Why don't you and Butch leave right now, Tom?" Mama suggested shakily.

They scrambled for the door, jamming into each other as they pushed through it.

Papa dropped the gun with a clunk on the polished floor of our hall and sat down next to it with a vacant look on his face. Mama stood over him, her face drained and empty.

Papa looked slowly up at Mama and said, "There is something we have to do. Come, Lea, Sara."

"What?" Mama asked, not moving.

He stood. "Come, come. We have to let everyone out! There are people who need to see the light of day."

He circled the house, turning on all the lights in every room. Mama and I followed him, holding hands silently. I noticed the gun lay stark and black on the floor of the hall. I wanted to pick it up, to stuff it in the garbage can, but I couldn't bring myself to touch it. So, there it lay.

"Now then, Lea, I need you to help me carry everyone out. You, Sara, gather all the tape you can find.

"What for?"

"Just humor me. You two do that very well." His lips turned up in the slightest smile.

Tape: in the kitchen, in my room, in the garage. I ran about and came back with an armload to find Mama and Papa stacking rolls of drawings in the hall.

"Here, Sara, these are yours."

"Are all these other drawings yours, Papa?"

"Yes. They are houses for everyone," he said. "Places where I thought each one would be safe and happy. There is even one for Ivan Watson. I'd like to send that plan to Billy and Eva."

It took us hours to unroll and tape up the accumulation of Papa's life. We forgot about dinner, we forgot about everything, except the drawings. Mama and I stood and drank in the range of Papa's work. There was the observatory for Rudi. There was a big mushroomy-looking structure for the digger. There were a few shadowy portraits, too, vague and dark, with such slight contrast it was hard to distinguish individual features. Was this the way Papa had visualized them in the dim light of the hole? What had he called them?

Shadow memories!

"Which house is for Ivan?" I asked, ignoring the voice.

Papa pointed.

"Why that one?" Mama asked.

"A man who wanted lots of children should have had a large house," Papa said. "I put in playrooms and a huge kitchen; a warm place where the family could sit and read. Ivan was a watchmaker, so I put in a workshop. And see, right there, a fanciful playground for his children!"

"It's beautiful, Papa. Would you mind if I hung something next to Ivan's house?"

"What is it, Sara?'

I got my drawing and held it up.

Papa pointed to the shadowy figure of himself. "Is that me?"

"Yes," I said. "The way I thought you felt when you met Ivan."

"Almost gone," Papa said and nodded. "Yes, I was almost gone! Put it on the wall, Sara."

The phone rang. I looked at Papa. "It's Billy," I said. "Do you wanna get it?"

He moved his head very slightly and went into his office to pick up the extension, closing the door behind him.

Mama and I waited and waited. We heard him hang up, but he didn't come out. I paced the rooms of the house looking at the walls. Light fell on my father's world. A dark world full of death had brought to life an array of habitats I doubted anyone else could have imagined. My own drawings were stacked in a corner. I unrolled them and taped them into any empty spot I could find. That was when I noticed that Eugene wasn't hung on the walls with the others. Where was he?

"Mama, what's Papa doing in there?" I asked nervously.

"I don't know. We'll give him a few more minutes." Mama waited tensely, finally sitting stiffly in a chair by the stairs.

The sound of the clock was surprisingly loud. I could taste the tension and the fear in the air. Were the faces on the walls filled with fear at being in the light? Were they holding their breath? Were they waiting for the soldiers to come? I twirled from wall to wall, caught in the stares of the people Papa had come to know so well. I went up close and peered at the homes Papa had designed for them. It was dizzying.

Mama stood and began moving through the halls, travelling the walls with her hand out, touching the air in front of each drawing. I saw the gun still lying on the floor. It had made so many holes in our lives. I kicked it hard, and it slid into the wall and rebounded like a pool ball, coming to rest in a corner.

"Enough!" Mama said. "We go in and see what's happening!"

We walked in. Papa was at his drafting table.

"What on earth are you doing, Michel?" Mama demanded.

"I am finishing Eugene so he can come out."

Mama and I threw glances at each other.

"It's okay, Lea, Sara. I am okay."

He looked up. Tiny scraps of paper were sticking to his hands. One had floated up and landed in his hair. He swept it off and grabbed it as it glided away. "I am not sure I can make him completely whole again, but I must try."

Mama went up and rubbed his back, then leaned over and kissed him. He wrapped his arm around her waist. The glint of Ivan's watch fell on her cheek. She laid her head on his shoulder.

I left them there in the study. The house was eerie with its walls lined and covered in my father's dreams for the family he had made up and lost, just as surely as he had lost his real family. Time had stopped in our house. It hung in the air, and we were all caught between worlds. I had to get out of there.

I tiptoed through the back door and as soon as my bare feet hit the cool, damp grass, the world came roaring at me, all of its sounds magnified. Something slid through the grass. Harriet whispered on her back porch with her girlfriends. A car engine turned over. A train called distantly in the night, *whoo-ooo, whoo.* The wind brushed the branches of the trees and a night raptor lifted off, flapping into the air. Out of our house, life in real time flowed fluidly forward.

I climbed the tree house ladder. Something was up there moving around. "Willie?"

"Is that you, Sara?"

"Yeah. What're you doing up here, Willie?"

"Aw, I guess I'm pouting. My dad decided not to build the music room. I'm never gonna get to do what I want."

I sat down next to him. "Willie, my Mama wants to put my Papa in an institution."

"What? That's crazy!"

"See, that's the problem. Sometimes Papa is crazy."

"I think your father is great! I wish he was my father."

"Really?" I asked. "Well, that's because you've never seen him when he doesn't know the war is over."

We didn't say anything for a while, each of us lost in a grief of our own. Then Willie asked, "Sara, is your father really that sick?"

I didn't know. How could I? Nana said he had a big wound that wouldn't heal. And if it did, would it change him? My mind twisted around the issue, backed up, looked at it this way and that. I looked for a perspective that I liked, but I couldn't choose one. Each one had some part to it that scared me.

"Hey, Sara, we've been in the tree house a really long time. I think I'm gonna get something to eat and then bring my sleeping bag up here and spend the night. So if you need me, I mean if things get worse in your house, you'll know where I'll be. If you need me."

"Thanks, Willie."

We climbed down and I tiptoed back inside. As soon as I padded into the hall, barren walls screamed out at me and slow-motion overtook me again. The lights blazed brightly, but the drawings were gone. All that was left, hanging in lonely isolation, were the designs for Mama's house and Willie's music room and my swan-drawing of Mama. A wrenching pain twisted my stomach. Where were the other drawings?

I opened the study door. They were just as I had left them, Mama still sitting in a chair next to Papa, her head resting on his shoulder as he sorted through the scraps of Eugene's face.

Anger overwhelmed me. I was angry at Mama, at Papa, at being their child. I was angry because Mama didn't want to tell Papa about the new baby. I was angry that the war had twisted and crippled my father. All it had left us were his imaginings, and now even they were gone.

"Where are my drawings?" I demanded loudly, fracturing the frozen air around them. "And where are Papa's drawings?"

Papa and Mama looked at each other. Mama stood and pulled me out of the study.

"Sara, Papa put your drawings in your room. And his—he is going to offer them for sale at a gallery."

"What? Why! Why would he do that?" My hands were shaking and I felt like the room was spinning.

"Sara, you have to understand. Papa is trying to heal. His drawings, they're amazing and beautiful, but they were drawn for the dead."

"You said they weren't real! You said all of Papa's stories were made up! You said he was crazy! How can imaginary people die? Tell me how, Mama!"

"Papa is trying to give them a burial."

"What about my drawings? Does he want me to bury them, too? Some of them are of people from the hole!"

Papa was standing in the doorway. "Lea, let me talk to Sara alone."

Mama nodded and went back into the study.

"Sara, you must keep your drawings. They are beginnings for you. But for me, the drawings from the closet are endings."

I hung my head. "They're so beautiful! How can you sell them?"

"It's hard," he said sadly. "They were for my friends, but I can't keep them any longer. I have to let go of them, or I am going to be buried alive again. Do you understand?"

"Sort of. Do you have to send all of them to the gallery?"

"Sara, remember you said I had to make a choice? Well, I made it. Mama told me about the baby, but I can't stay with the three of you and keep the drawings."

"So, if you sell them, you'll be okay, Papa?"

"I hope so, Sara. I truly hope so." He hugged me gently. "One more thing. Your drawing of Ivan Watson, it's the best thing you've done. Thank you."

He rejoined Mama in the study, but left the door open. I watched him sit down again, pull his chair up and begin picking through the bits of Eugene scattered on his desk.

I wanted him to keep all the drawings that had recently lined our halls, that I still saw when I closed my eyes. Instead he was keeping Eugene. I squeezed my eyes shut, but this time all I could conjure up were the three scant drawings out in the hall. I reluctantly looked back into the study and saw Mama pull up close to Papa and lay her head back on his shoulder.

My heart sank. Didn't Mama understand? Didn't she know? As long as Eugene was in the house, Papa wasn't safe. I wanted to do something, but what? Papa saw me and smiled.

"Aren't you going to sell him, too?" I asked weakly from the hall.

Papa frowned a little. "No, not yet. I must wait until I have completed him. You understand, don't you?"

"No, Papa, I don't! How can you send all the other drawings away and keep him? Tear him up, Papa! Get rid of him. Don't keep him!"

"Don't be silly, Sara. I can't let him go like this."

No! I wanted to scream out, but I couldn't make a sound. Breathe, I told myself, but I couldn't.

I darted out of the house, out into the fresh air, into the black night hung in cold stars. I choked as my lungs tried to expand against my will. I put my feet on the ladder to the tree house. I thought I was going to suffocate. Blood pounded in my ears and my throat tightened. *Don't breathe. Don't take a breath, don't make a sound,* the voice demanded.

My feet would barely stay on the rungs of the ladder as I forced myself to climb. Please be there, Willie! Please! But he wasn't. I sank onto the floor, and curled into a tight ball, hugged my knees and took a breath. Slowly my heart stopped pounding and my lungs expanded, once, twice. I lay there and in my mind, I saw Papa, working on Eugene, snipping and pasting, snipping and pasting, over and over. I walked around him, a ghost of myself, and watched. There was a big hole in the drawing where nothing was pasted. The empty space started to bleed, just to drip a little. Papa would wipe at it, then snip, snip. But every time he tried to fill in the hole, it bled and he would crumple the bloody scraps of paper in his fingers and throw them away. And then blood would ooze from the wound again. I heard him say, "I'll never finish it. There aren't enough pieces. Some are missing."

I thought of the pieces I had pulled from Papa's face and flung to the wind that night. And then I heard myself think, *He's waiting for Eugene. He's waiting so he can finally say a proper good-bye. But what then?*

"Hey, Sara, what's the matter, why are you all curled up?"

Willie's voice made me sit up with a jerk. Had I been asleep? Had the vision been a dream? "Sorry," I said groggily.

"Is your Mama still sending your Papa off?" he asked.

"No. No, not right now anyway."

"So your father is okay?" he asked as he laid his sleeping bag out and we sat on it, our knees drawn up to our chins, like two dolls on a shelf.

"I don't know. I don't think I'm ever gonna know for sure. I guess it's like my Nana says about stuff—time will tell."

"I guess. You gonna be okay?"

"I think so. I think I understand something now. Nana says that Papa has a big wound in him where the soldiers yanked something out and he can't get it to heal up."

"Does it bleed?"

"Willie, it isn't a wound you can see. It doesn't bleed real blood. The thing is, Mama wants it to be all closed up, but Papa has been afraid to let that happen, 'cause that would be like forgetting everybody who died in the war. All these years, he has been keeping it open just a little bit so he won't forget, but when it gets too big and bleeds too much, that's when it drives him crazy and he goes back to his hole to be safe."

"Wow, Sara, that's pretty deep!"

"I'm just trying to make sense of it, you know?"

"Yeah. Are you gonna go to New York if they accept you, I mean with your dad sick and all?"

I thought about that. Would I? "I think I will. I don't think Papa wants me to wait for him to get all better. I don't even know if he ever will be all better."

"I still think you're lucky to have him for a dad. He really believes in you."

"Do you know what he did? He designed homes for all the people who hid with him during the war."

"Really? Wow!"

I closed my eyes, and this time, I saw all the drawings up on the walls again. "And today, he covered the walls of our house with them. Drawing after drawing he had been making for years lined our walls. He had hidden them, hidden them away in the closet in his study, so they'd be safe; hidden them in the dark, sort of the way he'd been hidden in the dark, in the hole. I don't know how many drawings there were, but not one had color in it. Not one!"

"Can I come see?" Willie asked.

"They're gone! He took them all down and sealed them into boxes to send away to be sold."

"Shoot! I woulda liked to have seen them."

"Yeah, but guess what, Willie? He left my drawing of Mama up and added two from the flat files where he keeps his commissions. One is of the house he's been dreaming of for Mama. And you know what the other one is? Your music room!"

Willie's eyes clouded up. I thought of Mama sitting in the study with Papa right that minute. I thought of how frightened she was, but there she was, while he cut and pasted his life back together, with her head on his shoulder.

Willie took my hand and I laid my head on his shoulder like a twin to the image of my parents. After a few minutes, Willie said, "You know, Sara, I think your dad will be okay now, don't you?"

"I hope so," I murmured.

"Sara," Mama called at that moment. "Sara? Come in. It's time for bed."

"I'm coming, Mama."

Willie stood and gave me his hand and hiked me up. He leaned down, surprising me as he hesitantly touched his lips to mine and pulled back quickly. "I'll walk you to your door."

"Okay."

"Hey, Sara?"

"Yeah, Willie?" I said, luxuriating in the feel of grass on my bare feet and my hand in Willie's.

"Are you going to change your family history report?"

"Huh?" I had forgotten about it.

"Isn't it due at the end of the week?"

"Yeah, it is."

"So are you, I mean, gonna make it true?"

I thought about it. All the faces that went with all of Papa's stories flashed across my inner eye. Suddenly they weren't black and white images, they were in full color, flesh and blood. Brown eyes, blue and green. Fair hair and dark. Bug-eyed and bright-faced. Le Constructeur and Ivan and The Trickster. All laughing and talking as if they were everyday people.

"No," I said loudly. "No, I'm not changing a thing! It's all true, Willie. All those people, they were real for Papa. They were his family. I'm not changing a single name. But I am gonna draw pictures of them for Mrs. Bancroft."

That a girl, Lovely Lili whispered right by my ear.

"Goodnight, Sara, I'll see you tomorrow," Willie said.

"Okay, See you tomorrow, Willie."

Willie climbed back into the tree house. He waved from the window and disappeared from view.

Something brushed at my hair. I looked around. Nobody, but I knew who was there.

"I'll never forget any of you," I said into the quiet night air.

Thank you, thank you, thank you, thank you, Lovely Lili's hushed voice replied, and then faded away into the darkness.